# The Dying Horse

A Novella by

## Jason Jordan

*Jason Jordan* (signature)

02/24/12

MINT HILL BOOKS

MAIN STREET RAG PUBLISHING COMPANY
CHARLOTTE, NORTH CAROLINA

Library of Congress Control Number: 2011942431

ISBN: 978-1-59948-333-7

Produced in the United States of America

Mint Hill Books
Main Street Rag Publishing Company
PO Box 690100
Charlotte, NC 28227
www.MainStreetRag.com

# CONTENTS

# CHAPTER ONE:
# ERIK

The five of us are in the driveway in the early morning. Dad and Mom are packing the SUV, about to leave for Florida for a week, while my brother watches. My little sister Jamie is excited about the trip—she loves the beach—but my younger brother Josh isn't.

"Do I have to go?" Josh asks Dad. Josh is at the point in his life—thirteen—when he doesn't want anything to do with the family, except for me, the older brother, who seems cool at twenty-two. He's lanky in his gray T-shirt and khaki shorts, rubbing his short brown hair, and will be taller than Dad and me in no time. His acne's growing, too.

"I've already told you," Dad says.

"But Erik gets to stay home."

"Yeah, but I'm much older than you," I say, my arms folded, "and I have to get that freelance project done." I wipe the sleep out of my eyes, hoping the sunlight won't prevent me from getting back to sleep after they shove off.

"I bet the hotel has wireless," Josh says. He's still trying.

"I bet it doesn't," I say.

"Leave it alone, Josh," my Mom says. "If Erik doesn't wanna go, he doesn't have to. He can take care of the house.

And Erik, make sure you feed the cats, water the plants on the deck, cut the grass, and get the mail. That way we won't have to get somebody else to do it. Josh, when you're old enough to stay home alone, we'll let you."

"But Erik can watch me."

"Sorry, bud," says Dad, "but you're going. And you're gonna like it."

"Fine," Josh says. He gets in the rear passenger side of the Lexus and slams the door. He puts in his iPod earbuds and stares ahead. He was the one who wanted to fly, but Dad wanted to see the sights on the way to Florida.

Right after, Jamie walks into the garage from the house and out to the driveway where she hugs my waist.

"Bye," she says. I look down but all I see is her long brown hair. She has her face dug into my leg, so I release her grip and kneel to her level. She looks tired.

"I'll see you when you get back, okay?" I say.

She nods, still in her pink pajamas, carrying a stuffed pig named Oink.

"Go ahead and get in the car, hon," my Dad says. "We're ready to go."

Mom walks to me and we hug before she gets in the car.

"Looks like you're the man of the house this week," Dad says, walking up to me. "No parties." He looks like an older version of Josh. I got my Mom's looks—blonde hair, blue eyes, tan. I'm pudgy, too, despite my workouts.

"Yeah, right," I say, hugging him. "Call me when you get in tonight. I might be out with friends, though."

"Will do."

"Are you gonna drive the whole way there, or do you think you'll stop for the night?"

"I'm gonna try to drive the whole day, but I'm not sure I can convince your Mom to let me do that." Dad pulls a folded $100 from his pocket and hands it to me. "For food."

"Thanks. See ya later," I say. I wave goodbye to them as the car pulls out of the driveway and onto the main street of our subdivision Pleasant Hills. Before they're out of sight, I catch them all waving back.

I go back inside and upstairs to my bedroom. I'm glad I have blackout shades—it's much easier to sleep when the room doesn't feel like an oven. I hear my phone, which is in the headboard, vibrating. I take off my T-shirt and shorts—everything but my boxers—and get in bed. The phone says I have a text message.

"This sux," Josh writes.

"Haha," I write back. "Try to have fun and you will. Goodnight." I set the alarm for noon, shut the phone, and put it in the headboard. Later, when I hear the vibrating, I flip open my phone and dismiss the alarm, as usual. I turn over and sleep for a couple more hours until my phone vibrates again, waking me up. I answer it without checking to see who it is, which I normally don't do.

"Hello?" I say.

"Hey, Chief. You asleep?" my friend Nathan asks.

"Naw, I'm up."

"I know you were asleep."

"You're right. I was. I don't know why I always lie about it."

"You feel like getting a few drinks tonight? Celebrate your family being out of town?" he asks.

"Sure. That sounds good. What time?"

"Ten would rock. Get there early and stay late. How's about The Front Door?"

"See you there at 10."

"All right, buddy. Go back to sleep."

"Goodnight." I laugh.

By the end of the night, I'm so drunk that me and Nathan have to get a taxi to take us back to our places. I leave my car in The Front Door's parking lot.

The next day, I'm too hung-over to get up earlier than the afternoon. Usually I keep a bottle of water on my nightstand so I won't have to get up in the middle of the night to grab one from the fridge in the garage, where we keep all the bottled and canned drinks. I congratulate myself for my ingenuity and preventive measures when I wake at 3 p.m.—groggy and tired but with little trace of a hangover. I flip open my phone and see that I have a voicemail from Dad. He left it last night, but the bar's music was so loud that I didn't hear my phone ring. I slap my phone shut and place it in the headboard without listening to the message. Still in my boxers, I get out of bed, put on the shirt that's on the floor, and go to the bathroom.

When I get downstairs, my feet cause the hardwood kitchen floor to creak, although the floor is supposedly doubly reinforced and has a "silent system" in place to boot. Yeah, right. I notice that the back door is open, which I think is weird, but rationalize it as being a result of my drunkenness. I close the door and lock it, glancing around the room to make sure the TV, DVD player, surround sound, and other things robbers would steal are still here. They are. The bottle of Sailor Jerry's is on the stovetop because I evidently forgot to put it back in the freezer before I left for The Front Door. There's about a fourth of it left, which is worth saving for another night in the very near future. I pick up the bottle and examine it, wondering how much rum I drank.

There's nothing else to do but start the day, so I pop a frozen chicken dinner in the microwave, and pour a glass of orange juice—a beverage I drink for the vitamins, not the taste. Reminding myself that I have to be careful, I carry the glass of juice, the tray, and a fork to the living room to watch TV while I eat. After setting everything on the end table, I sit on the couch and grab the TV remote. It has cat hair on it, so I blow to get some of it off. I expect one of the cats to emerge due to the noise I'm causing, but none show up.

It's strange with my whole family gone. Typically there's always somebody around doing something. Either Josh is watching TV in the living room or up in the game room playing video games on his PS3, Xbox 360, or Wii. Jamie is literally all over the place, with a trail of cats following the leader. My parents are in the kitchen, living room, or downstairs office. Their bedroom, too, but only at night.

I shift my thoughts back to what I'm doing, realizing that I've eaten the whole frozen dinner and left only the watery residue on the bottom of the black tray's compartments. I turn off the TV, get up and walk to the kitchen to toss everything disposable in the trash, and slip the glass and fork in the dishwasher for future cleaning. It's then, glancing out the dining room window, that I see my oldest cat sleeping under the wicker loveseat on the front porch.

"Shit," I say. I'm angry with myself for leaving her outside all night. She opens her big green eyes—sensing motion, perhaps—and lets out a meow that I can't hear through the glass. She rises and stretches her back, her legs. I instantly feel bad that I neglected to let her in, but she seems okay. She meows when I open the front door, practically sprinting toward her bowl of food while I attempt to smooth over the situation.

"I'm sorry I left you outside mother kitten," I say. I wish she could understand exactly what I'm saying, but I know she can't. I've heard that pets can only comprehend tone and certain words, if they're conditioned to respond to them. I watch her eat for a little bit—chewing the food loudly and swallowing it in big clumps. I'm always amazed when my pets never choke on their food, because they eat so fast. Once satisfied, she licks her chops and trots over to the recliner in the living room. She's the thinnest and most agile of the three, and deftly jumps to the recliner's arm and circles before lying down to take a nap. I pet her head, but mostly her ears because they're so soft. She always seems to like it. She closes her eyes and nudges my fingers when I stop, encouraging me to continue. I head into the kitchen.

Then I hear a voice behind me, a voice I've never heard before, a woman's voice. I turn, but see only the sun beaming through the windows onto the cat. She's staring at me with her big green eyes, her tail wagging gracefully, yet erratically.

"What was that?" I ask aloud, thinking it impossible to hear anything but a meow, or a car, a lawnmower, a shout in the distance. I correct myself to make more sense: "Who said that?"

"I did. Sit down," my cat says to me. "I have something to tell you."

It's official—something's wrong with me. I do what she says. I sit on the end of the couch, adjacent to the recliner, and listen.

"Where are the other two?" I ask her, referring to my other cats—solid black females.

"They've already left."

"Left? How'd they get out?"

"You left the back door open, and they tore through the screen." I look to my left and see that the screen has a hole in it big enough for a cat to slip through. When I closed the glass door, I didn't even notice the hole.

"Where'd they go?"

"We're supposed to leave."

"Where are you going?"

"I don't know."

"Why are you leaving? Who told you to leave?"

"It's instinct. We're leaving. I've got the feeling that something bad is going to happen soon. I hope you'll be okay."

"Yeah, me too."

I know—after seeing her as I never had—that I'll never be able to cradle her again. It'd be weird for both of us, but I quickly snap out of my thoughts, knowing she'll be on her way soon.

"So," I continue, "this is goodbye forever then?"

"Yes, probably. I wanted to stay and let you know we were leaving, so you wouldn't worry."

"Well thanks. I'll really miss you all." She meows, jumps to her feet, and leaps through the hole in the screen door, like someone commanded her to do so. I'm convinced that something is happening. Or is about to. I wonder how I'll tell my parents and siblings that the cats are gone. How will I explain what happened to them without it looking like my fault?

An hour later, after I've had time to mull over what happened and gotten fully dressed, I gather all the cat stuff in the house, put it in a trash bag, and tote it to the garbage can out back. If I leave any of it around (food bowls, litter boxes, toys) I figure I'll get depressed, and preventive measures certainly don't hurt. I plan to call somebody because I want to have something to do tonight. I'm short on money, but because I live with my family, I don't have to make much for myself, and I think it'll do me good to get out of the house again. It'll take my mind off the cats.

Once I graduated from college with a History degree, which my friends said was useless unless I wanted to teach, I got on the Internet and found a part-time freelance job writing high school textbooks. I thought I'd have a project to work on while my family's vacationing in Florida, but I checked my e-mail last night before I went out only to find that the funding for my current project was suddenly cut. Thus, I find myself in an interim.

In my college classes, I started work on a book and ended up with 150 pages in Word, single-spaced. I didn't do anything with it, and I still haven't. I thought about self-publishing it—it's called *Take Care of Yourself and Each Other: The Unofficial History of The Jerry Springer Show*—but decided against it. It was too expensive with no one backing me, like a press or benefactor, and had I been set on releasing a book, my bank account would've buckled at even the thought. As a result, I would've had to resort to the evil of all evils: full-time employment at a crappy job.

The matter at hand is that I have nothing to do during my family's vacation, and since the cats fled, I'm 100 percent alone. That fact sparks me to check in on my family in Florida. They should've arrived last night, but I was out with Nathan and missed the call. Plus they don't condone my drinking, so if I'm drunk, I never answer the phone anyway. I sit on the couch, get out my cell phone and scroll through my contacts until I hit Mom's number. It rings three times.

"Hi Erik. How are you?" my mom says.

"Hey. I'm good. You?"

"Pretty good. We're driving to the beach today. The weather report said there've been some strange developments in the ocean, so we're gonna go to the beach today before the weather gets too bad."

There's a pad of paper and a black pen on the end table. I scribble on the pad's OppenheimerFunds logo while Mom talks.

"What'd they say was going on?" I never pay attention to the news, much less weather reports. A long time ago I decided that looking outside was a good enough weather report for me.

"They don't know. They said it looks like a bunch of tropical storms are forming. A lot of them, moving very slowly."

"Whaddaya mean slowly?"

"The weatherman said it looked like they were building momentum, but if they were going any slower, they wouldn't be moving at all."

"Sounds weird. Anything else going on?"

"No, not much. We went swimming in the pool last night. Jamie stayed in the pool for hours. Josh didn't want to swim, though."

"He's never really liked it since he was a kid."

"We're at the beach, honey."

"Okay. I'll talk to you later."

"How are the kitties?"

"They're good," I lie. "Same as always."

I want the conversation to last longer, because I'm bored, but it doesn't. For some reason, I never want to go on vacations. The house is unusually quiet with both the family and cats gone, and even useful noisemakers like the washer and dryer, dishwasher, and water softener haven't run since they left. Dinner's approaching, so I decide to see if my friend Matt wants to meet in a couple hours. Hopefully he'll be up for picking me up because my car's still at The Front Door, but if not, I know my friend Nathan will.

"Hey, man. You want to get something to eat later?" I say.

"Totally. I get off work at 5. I can meet you around 5:30. If my drawer's out of balance, then I gotta stay and find the outage. Banks get pissed about that sort of thing," Matt says.

"Can you pick me up?"

"Where's your car?"

"It's at The Front Door," I say.

"What happened?"

"Let's just say that me and Nathan got a little carried away last night. So how about The Bamboo Plant?"

"Sounds cool. I'll pick you up around 5:30. Adiós."

I pick up my hardcover copy of Haruki Murakami's *Kafka on the Shore* off the coffee table and resume where I left off earlier in the week. I glance at the grandfather clock, calculating how much time can be allotted to the book. I should jog prior to dinner, but after a night of drinking, I never feel good enough. Even walking sounds like too much work.

Matt's true to his word and we're at The Bamboo Plant before 6. Since we eat here frequently, it's become our unofficial restaurant. It's easy to tell that it's locally owned and operated. The dining area has several small rooms, and the decorations match the Oriental setting, which the ubiquitous bamboo complements. In fact, it used to be a house, but was turned into a restaurant when new businesses sprang up beside it.

We walk in and the greeter seats us immediately.

"So, my family's on vacation in Florida," I say.

"Sweet. Time to party hard, huh? How long are they gonna be gone?"

"They'll be gone a week. It's been just a couple of days since they left. They went to Orlando, but they'll be going other places, too, like Daytona Beach. They're there today."

The waitress brings me the Diet Coke I ordered and I drink from the straw. "Say, I wanted to ask you something since you're into weather. Have you seen what's been going on with the—"

"Tropical storms? Yeah, I've heard about them."

"What's going on with those?"

"It's weird, dude. They're getting bigger. They're all gathered in the Atlantic and Pacific, but the strange thing is that they're barely moving. It's like they're waiting to fuck us up or something."

"Some people probably think it's the end of the world." I force a laugh that subsides into a fake grin.

"Yeah." He scoffs, loosening his tie. "We'll just have to wait and see what happens. Might be Katrina part dos. The worst would be if they started moving all at once—each in a different direction—and then crashed into different places. The wind patterns shouldn't allow that kind of thing to happen, but stranger things have happened. I'm sure your family will be fine in Orlando. Or if the storms turn into hurricanes and start heading toward Florida, they'll have enough time to evacuate."

"Should I be worried?" I say. I'm fiddling with my straw's wrapper, folding and unfolding it.

"I wouldn't be. Your family's smart. They'll leave if they need to."

"You're prolly right." He's always been a reassuring person, which is why I called him in the first place. "Are you working tomorrow morning?" I ask, trying to change the subject and get a feel for if he'll be up for drinking.

"Eight in the fucking morning."

"Banker's hours, huh?"

"Banker's hours don't exist anymore. Bankers work longer hours than they used to, and for less pay, but it pays the bills. Barely."

"Yes it does, plus you're able to live on your own. The whole 'self-sufficiency' thing. So you wouldn't be up for a drink or two tonight, then?"

"I wish, dude, but I can't. I gotta get up early for work, and if I drink, I'll smell like beer all day tomorrow. What about Nathan?"

"I'll call him. We went out last night, so he might not be up for another round. I'm already getting bored of staying at home since there's no one else there."

"At least you have cats."

"Yeah," I say, not lying exactly, but not telling the truth either. "Speaking of, have you heard anything about animals disappearing lately?"

"No," he says, looking confused. "Can't say that I have. Where'd you hear about that?"

"Oh, nowhere in particular. I was just wondering. Saw something on the news about it," I lie. Maybe no other animals left. Maybe they aren't going to. Maybe just mine did.

At the end of dinner, Matt offers to take me to my car, but I tell him not to worry about it because The Front Door is half an hour away. I'll get my car tomorrow, which will be an excuse to get together with somebody. If no one's available, I'll get a taxi again.

On the way home I think about places I can go, things I can do, people I can see, and when money's tight, that doesn't leave a whole lot of options. I suppose I can stop by a coffee shop and read for an hour or two, but I remind myself that I don't have a book on me, so I'll have to buy one—a used one since they're cheaper—before I go somewhere to read. And I don't have my own car, so I'd have to catch a ride from someone. If I go home to retrieve a book, then darting off again would be like a chore rather than an escape. And the car dilemma screws me over in that situation, too.

"Must've cost you a pretty penny, that cab ride," Matt says, ending my trance.

"It did. Say, would you mind stopping by the liquor store on the way? I'd like to stock up for the rest of the week."

"No problem, señor."

At the liquor store, I take my time and get something decent that will last a long time, or *should* last a long time. I settle on a bottle of Woodford Reserve—Kentucky bourbon. Rum's my favorite liquor, but I choose bourbon for a specific reason. Though I like the taste enough to drink it occasionally, it's also kind of revolting, so I conclude that I'll drink less of it than its better-tasting alternative. Either way, since I drank a lot last night and have hours upon hours in front of me, things will probably take a turn for the worse regardless. Drinking passes the time, gives me something to keep my hands busy with.

The old bald clerk says nothing to me except the total price, and I hand him enough cash to cover the bill. It's always cold in the liquor store. The fluorescent lighting reminds me of a supermarket. But without the people milling about, the electronic beeps of the registers, and the announcements blaring on the intercom, it seems like a dying one soon to go out of business. In spite of the store's unappealing qualities, the bottles of liquor and beer look delicious. I leave the store partly disappointed because although I'll enjoy myself, it's as if the choices I make can only be evaluated after sampling the other options.

At home, I type in the garage door code and the garage door rattles when it shuts. I briefly wonder what a defective one would sound like because one in perfect condition still makes a ton of noise. I guess the clanking of metal can only be so quiet. My keys hit the counter with a clink, and I survey the kitchen and living room, deciding where I want to spend my time. Despite the diversions I can line up—I really should work out—there are a few hours before it'll be late enough to meet up with Nathan. We usually meet around 10 p.m. on nights we hang out, though I figure calling him to set it up isn't a bad idea. I don't do it, though. Maybe I'm lazy or don't feel like spending the money on drinks when I just bought a bottle of whiskey. Nevertheless, my heart sinks at the prospect of spending the evening, and eventually the night, alone.

Having proposed and shot down avenues for entertainment—reading, writing, playing video games, watching movies, wasting time on the Internet—my mind turns to the one activity I was planning on engaging in anyway. I mean, aside from the stigmas and gossip that solitary drinking spawns, there's no one else around so I figure what the hell. Why not?

I sit on the front porch until night. Evening is dwindling and will soon give way to dusk. I'll go back inside then, when the mosquitoes, with their blood-sucking, clot-blocking ways, will be out in full force. There's a wicker chair on the porch, and I sit in it instead of the loveseat, which is directly across from the chair. I angle my chair so I'm facing the street, the houses across it, and the lake behind them. This way I can basically stare at any passersby who happen to wander along, whether they're cars, people, or geese. The bourbon isn't bad for being on the rocks, but I position the bottle behind one of the chair's legs to block it from the view of any would-be voyeurs. I only feel like looking slightly pathetic—not completely down and out.

Then the daughter of my next-door neighbor walks out her front door, up the driveway, and to the mailbox. Her parents must've forgotten to check today's mail. What day is today? I don't remember. They've been our neighbors for years, but I rarely see the daughter. Mandy is her name and she's one of the many girls who I continuously fantasize about. She's a little shorter than me with dark brown hair and eyes. Her toned, slender body speaks of regular activity, and more than likely, some affinity for a sport or two. On her MySpace she lists her body type as "slender," but I'd label it "athletic." I listed myself as "average." My Mom's slow metabolism works against me no matter how healthy I eat or how much I exercise.

Tonight she visits the mailbox in a pair of short shorts (the name brand emblazoned across her ass in all caps) and a tank top, which nearly reveals her twins. Her hair's pulled back into a bun, and her tan complexion only intensifies her aura. She looks good. Real good.

Luckily, Mandy doesn't notice me on the unlit porch when she walks to her mailbox, so I have plenty of time to plan what I'm going to say. The problem is that I'm pretty drunk, and know that I have the full potential to make an idiot out of myself with my inhibitions resting. I expect it — welcome it, even — because I have nothing to lose on a night like this. At any rate, I muster the courage to say something when she's on her way back in.

"Hey," I half-shout to her. It's a loud enough greeting to make it seem like I'm semi-interested in talking with her, but not especially heartbroken if she skips into the house without giving me any attention. I unsuccessfully try to suppress the antsy, tingling feeling that overtakes my stomach and groin when I see her.

"Hi," she says in a high-pitched tone, a tone I believe is an attempt to mask disinterest. She hops up the stairs — without pausing whatsoever — and goes inside.

"Fuck." I take another drink of whiskey to both console and contaminate myself. Later, twilight sets in, ushering in a host of nighttime sounds like the songs of crickets. Having drained a fourth of the bottle, I'm feeling pretty good and surprisingly not bored considering I'm just sitting around watching the scenery. The scenario I was hoping for is a long shot by anyone's standards—she's enthralled with me and has been ever since she first saw me, but hasn't had the courage to confess until now, when I have an empty house to myself—though I again know the highlight of the night will be an unsatisfying masturbation session prior to sleep. Disgusted with her, myself, everything in the world, I lumber inside. I lock the door, close the blinds on the main floor, and get ready for bed. I'll read until I get tired enough to sleep.

I'm not sure exactly when I fall asleep, but I'm used to rolling over multiple times a night to get comfortable, getting out of bed to use the restroom, or sleepwalking. Because my REM sleep is regularly interrupted, I often recollect my dreams in the mornings when I wake up for good. It's unsettling to think that dreams can occasionally predict the future. A combination of thoughts, hopes, and fears swirling in my head brews the most unnerving, faux scenarios. I can recall certain dreams with little effort—the result of such vividness. Sometimes it'll take all day to recall what I'd dreamt the previous night. Tonight's different because I can't shake the dream—nightmare, rather—I have about an hour before I plan to get up for the day.

The barn door opens with a loud creak and a thud. It's sunny, but intuition tells me that day will soon transform into night. I hear babies crying, though from the entrance I can't glance into the stalls, which line the barn's interior. Hay is everywhere, naturally, so I walk slowly to be quieter. This is when I notice I'm holding a sawed-off shotgun, ready to open fire at anything I cross paths with. The crying registers first, right as I gaze into the first stall. There are two babies hanging from large metal hooks that protrude through their eye sockets—now bloody, metal-filled holes. I can't stand the crying. Their screams are shrill and practically deafening, and my first reaction is to cover my ears, but thankfully my common sense kicks in and I hold onto my weapon. Tears pour down their cheeks, impossibly, as the bawling continues. There's no way to silence them. It's maddening. The blast and the resulting smoke are relief, oddly enough. I've shot them, splattering blood everywhere.

By the time I get to the last stall I look like I've swam in a pool of blood, the aftermath of laying waste to several pairs of babies. There are many, many stalls. And too much crying. I approach the last one with even more caution than the first. The final stall is the worst. I see the horse's head and gradually look upon his entire white body, lying on a pile of hay with short desperate breaths radiating at quick intervals. Horses don't lie down unless there's something wrong with them, or so I've heard, and I can tell there's a problem by the way he stares at me. His cold black eyes fixate on mine saying, *Get it over with. Go on. Get it over with.* The way he looks, struggling to catch every breath, is unforgettable, an image I try but fail to discard. I attempt to look away before I pull the trigger, but before I know it, I aim the shotgun and fire at the dying horse. On my way out, from the barn to the field, I fish my lighter out of my pocket and set the place on fire.

I awake to darkness—thank you, blackout shades—and the whirring of my small stationary fan.

# CHAPTER TWO:
# ERIK MEETS WES

I t's overcast today. The clouds are a dark gray, and I figure they'll let loose at any moment, unsurprising since it's rained every day this week at some point or another. After I use the bathroom, I fix a bowl of cereal and plop down on the couch, trying not to spill any milk. I always watch TV while I eat, so I pick up the remote and hit the POWER button, but nothing happens. I press it again to no avail.

"Dammit," I say, flustered. "Wait a second." I set the bowl of cereal on the coffee table, and reach to turn on the end table lamp. The ridged, black knob clicks, but the bulb doesn't produce any light. I walk to the refrigerator and open the door. No light here either, but due to the insulation, it's still cold inside and will be for a long time. "Dammit," I say again, thinking I have the culprit in mind. Our subdivision's power is always going out for inexplicable reasons. "It worked last night." A few days home alone and I'm already talking to myself.

Back on the couch, I eat my cereal in silence, looking at the TV as if it's on. I put the bowl on the end table and walk upstairs to my bedroom, where I'll try to get some more sleep. I lie down on my side and drift off.

I wake up later, not certain whether I've slept for minutes or hours, but it feels like hours. Curiosity gets the better of me, prompting me to check my phone, which I grab out of the headboard and flip open. Dead. Great. I forgot to charge it last night. I sit up to look at the clock on my desk, but it's still blank, meaning the power's been off since early last night.

I'm still in my room when I notice what sounds like a dull roar coming from outside. I raise my shades, but nothing seems out of the ordinary. I can't see too far in either direction, so I head downstairs to investigate.

I pass through the entry hall to the front door, open it, and slip outside. Though it's daytime, there's no direct sunlight coming from anywhere, except from the few rays penetrating the heavy cloud covering, which becomes more ominous as time goes by, like a bad storm's brewing.

I step onto my front porch and gaze toward my subdivision's entrance, hundreds and hundreds of yards away.

"Oh shit."

The crowd is thick and wide, and since our subdivision—the richest part of town—borders the poorest, I figure I know where they came from. They must've climbed over the gates and everything. Something big's going on. They're setting fire to the houses. Most of them are blazing. I see a bunch of people running off with TVs, jewelry, alcohol, and anything else they can carry. I notice a couple of bodies lying in the street. Are they unconscious or dead? Either way, I feel like I'm on a movie set. A few loud pops sound off, and then screams. Gun shots?

Then it dawns on me: they're headed in my direction and I have to get out of here. I jump up the porch steps, grab the bottle of bourbon I accidentally left outside the night before, and run inside. After locking the door, I set the bourbon on the kitchen counter and dart up the stairs to my room. From out of my closet I pull my dad's old duffel bag, which he used in the National Guard, and throw in some hoodies, T-shirts, pants, socks, and boxers, then get dressed—preparation for the weather conditions the clouds unknowingly predict. My backpack is by my desk, so I pick it up and empty it to make room for other things. There's nothing else I can do but make a run for it, or barricade myself in against the mob, but I'm not brave enough, or stupid enough, to seriously consider the latter.

Downstairs, I open the pantry door and stuff random boxes of food into the duffel bag, filling it to capacity. Perhaps it's my affinity for survival movies and TV shows, but I've always thought about what I'd need if I knew I'd be stranded on my own for an undetermined length of time. I even wrote a list once.

"Weapons. I need weapons."

Mom won't allow Dad to have guns in the house. We keep baseball bats in the basement, so I run down the stairs to the storage closet. I choose a wooden Louisville Slugger. There has to be more to choose from. Noticing the kitchen knife set when I'm back upstairs, I remove the butcher knife from the stand, pull the guard out of a drawer, put it over the knife, and toss it in my backpack, which I strap on. Still not good enough.

"I've got to get the hell out of here," I remind myself. I walk into the garage only to remember that my car's at The Front Door. "Shit!"

I glance at my Dad's blue toolbox, and before I'm ready to make my getaway, I procure a wrench, a can of mace, a flathead screwdriver, and a hammer. With the riot approaching, there's only one last decision to make—what do I do to the house? I'd rather see the house burn down than any of them get our stuff. And if they're going to burn it down anyway, I'd rather not let them have the satisfaction. I notice the bottle of bourbon on the counter. A Molotov cocktail? No, too difficult. The bourbon'll help do the job, though. If things go back to normal, we'll be able to collect insurance. I'll lie, say I left before the riot got this far.

I pour all the alcohol onto the kitchen floor. There's a half empty can of gas in the garage, so I bring it in and douse the living room floor. I hesitate when it comes time to actually set the fire. I'm not exactly sure how to set it safely, but I use a dishtowel. I light it with the lighter I keep in my pocket, and let the towel drop to the floor of the living room. The flames spread immediately. I do the same in the kitchen. It's too hard for me to watch, so I shoulder the duffel bag and make my way to the garage where I open the garage door to leave. For some reason I'm still compelled to close the garage door, which is as simple as inputting a code, so I do.

When I'm at the end of my driveway, I notice the threat has advanced quite a ways, though not far enough to pose a direct threat to me. I see neighbors in windows and doorways, holding shotguns and handguns, watching the rioters step closer and closer, preparing to make their stands against the mob. They're just things, guys. You can get new ones later. Maybe that hasn't registered with them, or just hasn't yet. I can understand wanting to guard your family, but what's stopping them from driving to safety in their SUVs? Those things can go off-road, avoiding the mob altogether. In any case, it only takes me a minute to reach the cul-de-sac, where I'll make my escape.

I look back one more time, prior to heading into the woods. I think about the whereabouts of my family and friends, if they're all safe, if they're thinking about me, too, hoping I'm okay. Time's wasting, however, so I tighten my grip on my duffel bag and head into the woods, knowing all the while that up ahead is the Interstate but dreading it just the same.

It begins to mist as I trudge through the woods. There's no way to avoid getting my tennis shoes soaked, and I don't own any boots, so I couldn't have been that prepared in the first place, even if there was time to dig through my closets. The onset of rain doesn't ease my mind either, because I'm not prepared for rainy weather. I don't have a tent. More importantly, I have no way to make a fire except for the lighter, which won't do much good in wet conditions. I suddenly halt and think about the gravity of the situation. It was pandemonium back there. My house is being destroyed, and I am the one to blame, though the looters would've gotten to it eventually. What's going on? Where are the cops? The military? Where am I supposed to go?

I set my backpack on the ground and rummage, hunting for the can of mace. Once I find the can, I zip up my pack, piggyback it again, and stick the mace into one of my front pockets. I'm naturally non-confrontational, and despite my reservations concerning physical violence, desperate times, as they say, call for desperate measures. If something or someone does attack me, then I'll at least be able to gain the upper hand with the mace.

The mist quickly turns to drizzle, and I hope that it won't rain any harder. Blazing a trail through the woods isn't as bad as I figured it'd be, though the absence of a path slows me down. I still like the sounds that result from my trip—crunching of sticks, rustling of leaves, and raindrops hitting the ground. The wooded area isn't big, however, which means I reach the clearing after a half an hour or thereabouts and stand facing the Interstate from the top of a small hill. It's one of the lesser traveled Interstates in Indiana. As far as I can see, although I have to squint due to the rain, there's nothing. No cars. No people. An abandoned highway looks odd, and because I'm used to vehicles bombarding this particular route during rush hour, the silence is unnerving. I expected to see a caravan fleeing the area, getting to safer ground. There'll be problems ahead for me. I'm sure of it. Even so, I make my way down the embankment.

I raise the hood on my sweatshirt as soon as the drizzle turns to showers—a grimy day that reminds me of autumn.

Dead leaves cake the ground and nearly cover the grass leading from the edge of the woods to the pavement of the Interstate. I cross the embankment and I'm fortunate to not slip and fall on the way. When I set foot on the barren Interstate, it seems like a scene out of a movie. It's almost like being on a deserted highway in the middle of Idaho, Montana, or one of those states in which cars are few and far between. For a second I imagine I'm a hitchhiker who no one'll pick up because I could be a serial killer or worse—whatever that would be.

I forgot to grab my binoculars, so the best I can do is stare and squint in either direction for a little bit, but no matter how hard I look, I see nothing except an empty road. I forgot my cell phone, too. It was dead anyhow. I reach into my pocket and palm the mace to reassure myself, and start walking down the side of the Interstate, in the opposite direction of my town. After about an hour of walking in the rain I'm thoroughly drenched, despite my coat, and am thankful to reach an overpass so I can stand underneath it for a while without continuing to get soaked.

There isn't much I can do without any transportation, and I feel like I'm not making progress, but then again, I'm not sure where I'm going. I set my backpack and duffel bag down and sift through the bag for a box of crackers and bottled water. It isn't a meal, exactly, but it's the best I can do. Sitting here watching the rain, I think about how it looks and sounds nice—until I gotta venture into it. Even though there's only a slight wind, I'm still cold, and the prospect of getting dry, or dry*er*, is gone. In any event, it's time to move on and hopefully by the time night falls, I'll find proper shelter in a warm dry place.

This blows, I keep thinking while walking sluggishly on what appears to be an endless road to nowhere. The rains haven't let up, nor have they intensified, but the constant down pouring is discouraging, as if everything needs to go wrong in accordance with Murphy's Law. Another hour passes with little development. As my motivation and morale decrease, so does my speed. Brisk walking turns to ambling, and if the road weren't my ostensible guide, then it'd look like I was wandering aimlessly. And really, I guess I am. I feel momentary excitement when the next overpass comes into view, but am disappointed when it's merely the same as the last one—a chance to rest from pounding rain, yet no one and nothing in sight besides the road flanked by woods on both sides.

After another break, I set off more determined to reach my destination than before, until I remember that I don't have a destination. I almost reminisce about my family and friends, but force myself not to. Whenever I become hungry or thirsty, I sate myself with what I've packed—peanuts and low-fat cookies. Sometimes, when I have to use the bathroom, I do it in the open on the side of the road. It's weird for me, but also kind of liberating because it's one of those mores I've never broken except when I was a kid too young to know better or feel embarrassment.

I walk until dark and then I walk some more. The rain never lets up, nor does the boredom. Eventually I decide that the next overpass will be my shelter for the night because I'm tired and it's hard to see. When I'm underneath it, I take off my wet clothes, dry off with a spare T-shirt, and put on dry ones. It feels great to be in a fresh set of clothes, especially since it seems like I've been taking a perpetual shower for the past several hours.

Unfortunately, I forgot to pack another pair of shoes. My sneakers are saturated and I'll be forced to wear them tomorrow. I'm thankful that I work out on a regular basis. If I didn't, then the few miles I walked today would've lowered my resolve to continue, likely resulting in blisters, too. For now, these shoes will have to do.

I have to sleep on the ground, of course, but that's all right since there's no standing water to speak of. I'm glad to be dry. I pile my wet clothes a couple feet away from me, and empty some clothes from the duffel bag, which will serve as a pillow, so I'll have something to cover up with. "Goodnight," I tell my backpack. It takes a long time for me to get to sleep, as the ground is uncomfortable, but I'm able to succumb to the urge later on.

The dream begins with me walking along a beach on an island in the ocean. I can't recall how I've been marooned on the island, though I infer that I'm either the sole survivor of a plane crash or a sinking ship. Palm trees litter the vegetation, and there are coconuts scattered among the shaded portions of sand, which contrast with the outcroppings of rock that riddle certain parts of the coast. All at once I fondly remember books and movies that make use of the same debacle: *Lord of the Flies, Robinson Crusoe, Swiss Family Robinson, Cast Away.* I'm on the beach trying to conjure all the trials-and-errors that the characters from each underwent to minimize my failures, ensuring self-preservation. *How to Make a Fire, How to Open a Coconut, How to Build a Raft, How to Mend a Wound, How to Hunt*—books I'll write after I'm rescued.

In this particular dream, however, not much happens. I'm on the beach in tattered clothes, watching the horizon, treasuring the gentle breeze. The sun's beating down as if it holds a grudge, but the weather's nice, except for the fact that the tropical climate will last the entire year if my attempts at being noticed flop. I compare eternity to that deserted island. I notice my three cats running in the distance and they're having trouble navigating the soft sand. They're playing with each other like nothing's wrong, like nothing's wrong at all, and I don't question how they got here, even if I should.

I sleep lightly because the ground's uncomfortable. As far as I can tell, the rain continues pouring throughout the night, a steady stream of water that will probably lead to flooding in parts of the state. I'm not worried about it since I've never experienced a flood in my life. When I wake, I roll over and try to regain comfort, as hopeless as it feels sometimes, and doze off until I'm roused again. It gets lighter come dawn, but the dark cloud cover and rain block most of the sunlight, which keeps things overcast and gloomy.

Sometime in the morning or afternoon—I'm not sure which—I feel something nudge my arm. I keep my eyes closed and ignore it, praying that I'm in the middle of a dream, but sure enough, I'm nudged again, like something is poking me to see if I'm dead or alive. I open my eyes and see a guy, in a T-shirt and jeans, towering over me, holding a tire iron, rain running down his face. Even from a few feet away his arms speak of strength with numerous, spidery blue veins crawling every which way, housed by his muscular frame. He has long, curly brown hair pulled back behind his ears—further accentuating his cheekbones and jaw line—and if I had to guess, I'd say he's a few years older than me.

I'm confused at first, thinking I'm still dreaming, but then I panic, convinced he's going to hurt me. I slide back to the wall of the overpass and reach into my pockets for the mace, but am more afraid when I realize I left the can in my wet pants I took off last night.

"Woah, woah, man," the guy says, lifting his free hand in what I interpret to be reassurance. He has to yell due to the rain. "I'm not gonna hurt you. Just figured I'd check and see if you're all right. I'm Wes. Who're you?"

"Erik," I say.

"Pleased to meet you, Erik." He extends his right arm and we shake hands. "Now, where are you headed? Looks like you're running away—not that anybody can blame ya. Not in a time like this."

"Time like this?"

"You mean, you haven't heard?"

"Heard what?" I ask, genuinely perplexed. I think maybe he's referring to the riot.

"You haven't heard anything?"

"No."

"We're screwed, man. Those hurricanes hit everything. And that caused a shit ton of other natural disasters. Everyone's been without power for at least twenty-four hours. I think it went out about 4 a.m. yesterday morning. I was awake. I was up watching TV."

"Really?" I said. I wasn't questioning him so much as coming to a grim realization. "My family's in Florida."

"Sorry to hear that, but I'm sure they'll be okay if they evacuated."

"I hope so. Anyway, I walked for a long time yesterday, but never saw a car."

"Accidents. There are accidents all over the place— overturned semis blocking lanes, fires, carjackings. I think most people are too afraid to leave their houses."

"How'd you manage to get on the road?"

"I live right beside the Interstate, so I had no problem getting on it, and I guess I'm lucky since I didn't run into any accidents or anything like that."

"Yeah. I guess so."

"You need a ride?" he asks.

"Where are you going?"

"I don't know. Away from here. That's the plan."

"Thanks, but I don't know if I can trust you yet— especially with that tire iron."

Wes looks at the tire iron in his hand as if it just materialized.

"Oh this? It's nothing. I was just being careful, sneaking up on you like that. You could've had a gun or a knife or something. You never know, right? And what makes you think I should trust you?"

"Good point. Safety in numbers. Why didn't I hear you coming?"

"I don't know. My lights were on, but the rain's so loud it drowns out everything else. By the way, you can put your stuff in the backseat—wherever you want. I don't mind."

"You have a cell phone?"

"No," Wes says. "I don't think it'd do a bit of good if I did. I tried to use the phone—my landline—a few hours after the power went out, but it was dead. Radio's not transmitting anything either."

"That's the strangest thing I've ever heard. You have a computer?"

"No."

I wonder: Who doesn't have a computer these days?

I get up and put everything back into my duffel bag that I'd left out during the night. Yesterday's clothes are still damp, but at least they aren't soaking wet anymore. I hate to get wet again, as if there's any other choice, so I jump in the passenger side of his sky-blue Honda Accord as fast as I can. I shove my bags into the backseat while Wes situates himself. The tire iron's gone, and I assume he laid it down beside him just in case he needs it.

Wes starts the car and looks around the dash.

"What's wrong?" I ask.

"Nothing." He turns on the headlights. "Can never remember how to turn the lights on."

"Thanks a lot for helping me out," I say after a few minutes in the car.

"Not a problem. You'd have done the same for me."

Maybe, I think. Maybe not. I ask him about the radio, but he reminds me that it doesn't work. Every station is static.

We continue to pass the bleak, dreary landscape as the rain pounds Wes's car. I've stopped dripping by now, thankfully, and the heat feels good even though I know its attempt to dry me will be futile. Though Wes's news tugs at my conscious, I push the thoughts and memories of my family and friends to the back of my mind, so I can recall them in better times. I hate to admit it, but it seems I, or we, are at that point where self-preservation begins to take hold, where it becomes the number one priority. After all, things don't look good, and I only expect them to get worse, but Wes's presence calms me, knowing that we're stranded together.

I notice a magazine lying face down on the floorboard. I lean down, pick it up, and turn it over.

"*Good Housekeeping*. You a fan?" I ask Wes. He looks at it and laughs.

"Oh that. Uh, my ex-girlfriend must've left that in here. We weren't dating, but I dunno. It was fucked up."

"She leave that, too?" I point to the container of scented lotion next to the emergency brake handle.

"Yep."

Needless to say, I suspect Wes is lying about this being his car. Fumbling for the lights, and having a women's magazine and a bottle of scented hand lotion doesn't add up. I'm apprehensive about pressing the issue, so I decide to beat around the bush rather than dive right into it.

"Anything in the trunk?" I ask.

"I don't remember. It's been a long time since I've gotten into it." The tire iron says otherwise. Who doesn't keep their tire iron in their trunk? "Why do you wanna know?" His eyes meet mine. There's a moment of awkward silence.

"For my bags." I point to the backseat where they're piled. I'm relieved that I came up with that so quickly.

"Next time we stop I'll pop 'er."

"Thanks."

Minutes later, Wes says "Hey," aware that I'm lost in my thoughts. "It looks like there's something up ahead. Probably not good, whatever it is."

He slows down and we strain to see what or who is in the distance. The rain obscures my view too much to decipher anything, and I'm careful about getting too close. In any case, if someone's looking in our direction, they've already spotted us and will be prepared to defend or attack—depending on what they want.

"We better pull off," I say, "before we get too close to 'em."

"Okay."

"I mean, we should pull to the side of the road, get out, and approach whatever it is from different spots, unless you have a better idea. I've watched a lot of war movies, so I guess I have some idea of what I'm doing."

"I like your thinking, Erik. You can be the leader, plus your plan's better than busting through or driving around a roadblock, if that's what it is. This car's great, but won't make it very far in the mud. Unfortunately I only have a half tank, which'll last for a while, but not long enough. That's for damn sure."

Wes pulls to the side of the road, turns off the headlights, and shuts the engine off. He leaves the keys in the ignition.

"So, what do we do?"

"For starters, you could grab your keys."

"Shit, right."

"Do you have anything you could use as a weapon in here besides the tire iron?"

"I don't think so."

"Eh, too much effort to get all my supplies out of the back, plus they might notice us even more if we don't dart off to opposite sides of the road, as we prolly should. You can use the tire iron. I'll use something else." I grab my backpack from the backseat, twisting and contorting my body uncomfortably to reach it, and sift for a weapon. I settle on the butcher knife, but leave the guard on so that I don't accidentally cut myself.

"Won't these get slick in the rain?"

"Everything gets slick in the rain."

"Good point. So, uh, what are we gonna do again?"

"Once we get out of the car we'll run to opposite sides of the road and start walking toward whatever it is that's up ahead. Walk on the side of the road so you'll be harder to see, especially with the rain. We'll just have to try and see each other from the other side and come together when we reach it. Be careful."

"Have no fear, fearless leader," he says, and then salutes. I can't ascertain whether he's mocking me or simply acting goofy.

After getting out of the car, we sprint to opposite sides of the road. The rain is falling heavily, soaking us quickly and easily, and it's difficult to maintain decent visuals in such inclement weather, with distance further hampering us. I motion to Wes to move forward and we edge closer to whatever it is up ahead. The closer we get, the more I have an idea of what it was. It appears to be a massive pileup with a couple overturned semi trucks at the front of the mess—perhaps the cause of the accident. All the engines are off and there's no smoke, making it seem as if a significant amount of time has passed since the accident took place. If there was a small fire, the rain would've extinguished it.

Wes and me eventually agree it's all right to converge at the scene of the accident because there's no trace of life. In fact, there's no trace of any movement whatsoever. I peer into the cab of one of the overturned semis—broken glass is everywhere—and see a corpse splayed across the seats. I immediately avert my eyes like it's a reflex. There's no point in checking to see if anyone in the five vehicles are still alive. We can't contact anyone, and the passengers who aren't dead evidently left the scene a while ago, wanting to dodge responsibility and flee to safety.

We're silent while we survey the damages, until I speak up.

"What do you think?" I ask, not knowing what else to say.

"Fucked up. The people who didn't get fucked up are long gone."

"Yeah, but why would they leave? You can go to jail for leaving the scene of an accident. What's it called—hit and run?"

"You gotta remember that we aren't exactly in an everyday situation here. I bet the President's declared a state of emergency, or whatever that warning's called, since everything's so fucked up. People are getting robbed and carjacked too, so it's not safe to be out on the roads. They're deathtraps, basically. I don't want to think of this as *Mad Max* on steroids, but it might be. Obviously no one can get through here with the pileup, and there's gotta be something blocking the other direction, which would explain why we haven't run into any cars yet. We need to figure out where we're gonna stay for the night, and where in the fuck we're headed."

"What about your house? You said it's a few overpasses down."

"Nah, I ain't going back there. It was starting to flood when I left. I don't wanna see my possessions go down like that. It'd be like starting over for me. I left from there. Let's try somewhere else."

"It's a stupid question, but your car can't get around this wreck can it?"

"No way. With this rain and mud, there's no way I'd be able to get that Honda to do anything but get stuck."

"Right. I didn't think so. I guess we're just gonna have to head the other way, down the Interstate, and if we come to a blockage, or whatever, we'll have to take an exit and see what we can find."

"Where are we going?"

"I don't know, but I'm getting soaked. Let's get back in the car."

"Yes, sir."

As we drive, we draft a plan. "What do you think?"

"I haven't decided," Wes says. "You still have family and friends, but you aren't sure about where they are?"

"Yeah."

"All I've got is me. I live by myself."

I think of my family. Where are they? What are they

doing? Are they okay? I pose these questions to myself and answer them positively. Will I ever talk to them again? I want to believe I will, but I can't say for certain. I reminisce about my brother Josh, how he threw a fit before involuntarily leaving for Florida. He wanted to stay with me. How different would this have been if it were me and Josh? I can't imagine.

"I think we should head south," I say.

"Why south?"

"I'll be honest. Remember I told you my family's in Florida on vacation."

"Where in Florida?"

"Orlando. Also, the farther south we go, the warmer it will be. You have any objections to that?"

"Sounds good to me, but it'll be dark soon. We should look for somewhere to shack up for the night. The fucking rain isn't going to let up. We'll have to deal with that shit, too. Say, there was a gas station off the exit we just passed. We could sleep there. Stock up on supplies."

"We'll need to get dry no matter what, and get something to eat as well."

"Say no more, General. Shouldn't take too long."

The exit comes quicker than I anticipate, and I'm thankful to be off the main thoroughfare. Contrary to what Wes was saying earlier, I'm skeptical about it being incredibly dangerous to be out wandering around. He made it sound like we're the only humans left, like in a zombie movie, like everyone else is out for our brains. Still, I don't want to go anywhere without preparing beforehand, so I agree that we should take our time and set off once we're more ready to tangle with threats, bear the elements, and, most importantly, figure out where we're going. Orlando is the provisional destination.

"That's the place you want us to stay at?" I ask, hoping it isn't. Right off the exit there's a gas station that looks like it was deserted long ago. In the twilight its broken glass, faded vandalized signage, and weed-strewn dirt cast an eerie mood. Even an experienced haunted house crew—used to making a place spooky—couldn't have done a better job.

"Nah, that ain't it. It's the one down the road."

"Good. That place looked messed up."

"It's been abandoned for a while. No one thought it was worth fixing up and reopening or selling. Piece of shit town."

We have to break a window, but we get in the other gas station without much trouble. It's been deserted since the storms starting coming through, Wes tells me, and all the electricity is off, so there's no way to get any gas from the pumps, or keep anything cold in the fridges and freezers. In order to not draw attention, we park the car in the grass behind the station. We throw our stuff through the window, and then I hoist Wes up so he can get inside. The front door is locked—the last person to leave locked it behind them, I bet. Wes lets me in and I lock the door.

The place is probably as organized as it was when it was open since nothing seems to be in disarray. The first order of business is repairing the window I broke. Wes grabs a roll of duct tape from one of the aisles while I procure a flattened, cardboard box from the storage room. Once taped up, the window isn't letting in air or rain. We aren't dry by any means, and the night is sure to be colder than optimal for sleeping outside or even with just an open window. The flashlights prove useful—we "borrow" the flashlights and batteries from the store—but after searching for anything of value and finding nothing out of the ordinary, we sit on the floor eating whatever food we can scrounge up—energy bars, chips, and drinks.

"We should probably stock up before we leave," I say between mouthfuls of a PowerBar, which I wash down with lukewarm orange juice.

"Okay," Wes says. He's devouring as much beef jerky as he can get his hands on—careful not to eat two of the same flavor in a row. "You think this milk is still good?" he asks, holding onto one of the fridge door handles.

"I wouldn't drink it."

"Okay." He drinks soda instead, inadvertently reminding me to brush my teeth and take extra toothbrushes and toothpaste for the road.

Eventually, knowing we'll have to sleep, we tote more flattened, cardboard boxes out of the storage room and place them on the tile floor to function as pseudo-mattresses. Fortunately there's a blanket display, which we dismantle to make our respective beds. I hate sleeping on a bare floor, even if there are cardboard boxes to cushion it. Then we change clothes—each takes a turn in the bathroom and leaves a flashlight on to see—and drape our wet clothes over shelving to dry. The rain let ups once darkness settles in, but in the distance there's lightning, intermittently flashing to warn of other storms headed our direction. In fact, there's not much else to do but watch the outside.

Following a long bout of silence while observing the lightning, I say to Wes, "I hate to sound all paranoid and stuff, but we should probably sleep with weapons at our sides—go military, I guess."

"Affirmative, General. I'll keep the tire iron."

"I've got the knife, plus some other stuff. It feels a little early to sleep, but I'm tired, so I'm gonna try. What about you?"

"I'll lay here until I fall asleep. There's nothing else to do, eh? Let's talk about where we're headed in the morning. I don't feel like getting into all that now."

"That's fine with me. It's not like we don't have the time. Remind me to pick up some maps before we leave. I'm sure they're around here somewhere. Wake me up if anything happens." I don't expect anything to happen with no sign of the car or us from the outside.

"Affirmative."

"Night."

I close my eyes, dreading the inevitable but succumbing to it just the same. I ponder about how Wes has been addressing me lately. Should I bring it up? Ask him if he's making fun of me? I always do this: I think about a decision I have to make but fall asleep before I'm able to come to one.

During the night I keep tossing, turning, and waking up—partially due to the discomfort and partly due to the uncertainty the situation has spawned. What I wouldn't give for an actual bed.

Brains never rest completely. They never shut down, not even for a moment. All the day's events continue sloshing around inside my mind, and are relived, reinterpreted, or filed away as my brain waves steady for sleep.

I'm wading through the water and reach shore shortly after the dream begins. The jungle is dense except for the shoreline, which appears to be the only part left uncovered. It's daytime. I can't locate the sun, but the heat is almost palpable, as humid as Hell itself. I've never subscribed to the theory that Hell can be a particular state of mind. Deep down I know it exists—a living, breathing place that feeds off the souls of the damned, writhing in agony, wailing for a savior, repenting too late. Could it be a pool of raging fire and brimstone? Or is it calm and serene like the jungle, but with unbearable humidity? I don't know.

I'm on the shore surveying my surroundings. It's busy in the jungle. The sounds of tropical birds and insects radiate from locations I can't pinpoint. The silent creatures lurking about are the dangerous ones, however, and won't alert me to their presence until it's too late.

"We should get going."

I look in the direction of the voice and am surprised—elated—to see the mother kitten. She's just as I remembered her—all black, green eyes, tail wagging unpredictably.

"Where have you been?" I ask.

"Here."

"In the jungle? Where'd you go after you left the house?"

"I live here now. I've been instructed to guide you."

"By who? God?" I snicker.

"Not exactly. Follow me."

"Wait," I beckon as she trots off into the underbrush, "where are the other two?" But she isn't listening.

I hear a cough and open my eyes to darkness, and try to see the figure more clearly while they adjust.

"Are you all right, man?" I ask Wes, who's evidently on the tail-end of a coughing spell.

"I think so. I just hope I'm not getting sick."

I consider getting a drink of water, but decline as I'm groggy and afraid I won't be able to return to my dream. I roll over on the mat, turning my back to Wes, and try to regain unconsciousness.

"Where'd you go?" the mother kitten asks.

"I had something I had to attend to."

"Oh, all right. You froze there for a minute so I thought something was wrong."

"Nope. Lead on."

"The clearing is up ahead. It shouldn't take us too long to reach it."

I follow the mother through the thick growth, pushing my way past branches and carefully sidestepping obstacles on the ground. For some reason, perhaps oblivious or in shock at the sight of the locale paired with the reappearance of one of my former cats, I haven't noticed my garb, which is that of a stereotypical native. It seems I've returned to *Lord of the Flies*. Dressed in leaves with paint on my face (it rubs off on my fingers when I touch it), I find myself brandishing a spear in one hand while the mother kitten jogs at a comfortable pace, confident in her navigating abilities.

The clearing is circular in shape, and it seems a precisional force razed the plant life. It's manmade, undoubtedly, and in the middle of the jungle surrounded completely by flora.

"Your host will be with you soon. I'll see you later."

"Host?" By the time I say it, she has already darted out of sight. The word "host" unnerves me because I associate it with its more unsettling relative, "parasite." Suddenly, everything goes dark—black as pitch. I can't even see my hand in front of my face. A spotlight appears, and then I hear the voice of what sounds like a TV game show announcer.

"Are you ready to play *Who Gets the Ax?*" he shouts out of sight. The spotlight then flies to the left side of the clearing. On cue, a man in a suit with a shiny, gold halo hovering a few inches above his head jogs out from the underbrush.

"Hello ladies and gentlemen! My name is Jesus Christ, and I'll be your host this evening. Our contestant is Erik, and for his sake, let's hope he's ready to play *Who Gets the Ax?* Shall we begin?"

At this point the lights come on—despite being in a jungle that would be devoid of technology in the real world—and what I see looks exactly like the set of a game show, similar to "The Showcase Showdown" at the end of *The Price Is Right*. I see three figures behind their respective podiums, and am immediately nonplussed when I recognize them. There's no way of knowing why *Who Gets the Ax?* chose who they did, but I'm distraught when I see both of my dead grandfathers, and, to complete the line-up, the horse I killed in an earlier dream.

"All right, Erik," says Jesus Christ. "Choose who will get the ax. And let Me remind viewers at home that the term 'ax' is actually slightly misleading since Erik will be using a spear to service his target, but in My—excuse Me, Our—defense, let Me bring to your attention the title of our program. *Who Gets the Ax?* has a much nicer ring than *Who Gets the Spear?* Don't you agree? So, Erik, please choose your target, stand in the designated area, which, reminding viewers at home again, is fifty feet away from the target he will choose, and give it your best shot, er, toss!"

"I have to choose?" I almost shudder at the sound of my own voice, as if I expect a malicious, nefarious entity to be controlling me via telekinesis—an entity capable of engaging in such an activity without emotional baggage and morality coming into play.

"Yes Erik," Jesus says with a hint of impatience, "you must choose."

"And if I don't?"

"Death to all!" He exclaims, smiling afterward.

Before I'm fully aware of what's happening, I hurl the spear at the horse to the instantaneous, collective gasp of the nonexistent audience—a prerecorded track. Thrown with such great force, the spear punctures the horse's neck and slides straight through. Blood flows like water from a hose. The horse drops, emitting a thud, and I imagine for an instant that the earth shakes upon impact and then reverberates. Jesus' mouth is agape. My grandfathers are oblivious to the whole incident and continue to stare at me.

Jesus is the first to respond, through gritted teeth.

"You killed him!"

"You told me to!" I shoot back.

He grabs spears from nowhere and lobs one to each of my grandfathers. They begin walking toward me with spears in hand, ready to plunge them through my yielding flesh.

"You killed the horse!" Jesus yells again, the halo conspicuously absent.

I backpedal, shouting, "I didn't want to! I didn't want to!"

And then Wes is shaking me and yelling and I'm awake and it's all over.

# CHAPTER THREE: ERIK & WES HEAD SOUTH

hould we clean up?" Wes asks in the morning.

S "Nah, just leave it like it is in case someone else shows up. They'd prolly be glad to find our beds."

We're standing across from one another, and I briefly study Wes's stature. He's several inches taller than me, and, without a doubt, stronger. If it ever comes down to it—a versus match with high stakes—he'll overpower me with ease. I'd bet on him. Still, I hope it won't ever come to that because I'll have to resort to fighting unfairly by eye gouging, biting, and crotch kicking.

"What?" asks Wes.

"Oh, nothing. Sorry. I was just thinking about where we're heading."

"You wanting to go south to find your family? Where'd you say they were?"

"They're in Orlando unless they evacuated."

"You think they'll be there? We don't have enough fucking gas to get down there."

"I doubt they're there, but I don't know where else to go. We'll just have to find gas—maybe steal a car with more gas."

"Easier said than done, but you're the General."

"You got a better idea?"

"Nope."

We pack and take some extra provisions for the road. Wes unlocks the gas station door and we leave. I'm beginning to crave an actual meal—I'm sick of snack food—but am glad I have plenty of protein-loaded PowerBars and vitamin-rich orange juice. I figure I'll need them sooner or later. Thankfully, it's not raining.

Back on the Interstate heading south toward Florida, in the opposite direction of the wreck we encountered yesterday, I recall my dreams and ponder their significance. What could they possibly mean, if anything? I've never subscribed to the theory that dreams predict the future, though I suppose they could, nor do I think they're symbolic all the time, but maybe it's possible for them to be symbolic occasionally. Is there a way to be sure of their meaning? Freud might be able to answer that.

"I keep having this dream," I tell Wes. He evidently pocketed gum from the gas station and is chewing loudly. Sometimes he'll blow a bubble then pop it with gusto.

"That's annoying *and* bad for your teeth," I say.

"No it ain't," he says.

"What? Not annoying?"

"No, it's not bad for my teeth. I read on the box that this gum's got xylitol in it, which actually cleans teeth, so you're wrong."

"I'm half right—it's still annoying even if it isn't bad for your teeth."

"Half right, half wrong. Same shit," he says, pausing. "Point taken. I'll try to be quieter, General. Gum helped me quit smoking, so I chew it a lot."

"And why do you keep calling me General?" I ask.

"Cuz you are a natural order-giver." Wes lazily salutes. "I didn't mean to piss you off, if that's what I did."

"Naw, I'm just having a lil fun with you."

Before long, we pass the exit I take to get to my house. My house isn't there anymore, I guess. Part of me wants to see it. I imagine a huge pile of ashes, a driveway leading up to it. What would Dad and Mom say? It was their dream home, built according to their specifications. I'm hoping I'll see them again and be able to tell them about what's happened. Prayer might help. It couldn't hurt.

I snap out of my reverie, realizing that yesterday, a day spent walking mile after mile in the opposite direction, was an exercise in futility since we're backtracking today. I'm glad I jog three times a week in my home gym. Otherwise, I would've had blisters. I escaped the mob, so yesterday was good for something at least. It's reassuring to have a destination in mind now.

"So, you were saying."

"Oh, I keep having this dream. It's not so much a recurring dream as there is just a recurring character or animal or whatever you'd call it in the context."

"What kind of animal is it?"

"A horse. It's a white horse."

"What happens in your dreams? You don't fuck it, do you?"

"No." I swat at the air, dismissing his notion. "I always end up killing it. It doesn't seem like I ever want to, but I always do like it's automatic or something. The last one was crazy. I was on some weird game show and Jesus Christ was the host. Eventually he told me to kill the horse and I did—with a spear."

"Have you always had that dream?"

"It started recently. Since all this traumatic stuff's gone down."

"Could be your mind dealing with this fucked up shit. Everyone tells me it's strange that I don't dream."

"I bet you dream. You probably just don't ever remember your dreams."

"I don't know. You'd think it," Wes says but trails off.

"What?" I ask, looking directly at him as he drives staring straight-ahead.

"Look. Up there," he says.

I squint to distinguish what's in the distance, but can't make out any specifics other than a roadblock. There are a few orange and white wooden structures blocking the Interstate, so Wes slows down.

"I don't like the look of this," I say.

"Me neither. What else are we gonna do?"

"I don't know. I don't see anyone around."

"Famous last words, General."

I glance at Wes, meeting his eyes.

"It's habit at this point, General," he says.

"Fine," I say, apathetic.

We have reservations about getting out of the car, but besides driving through the barriers, there isn't anything we can do. The weather's cloudy—dark and ominous like calm before the storm—and despite being on an Interstate, we find ourselves alone. As we stand beside our respective sides of the car eyeing the roadblock, Wes brings to my attention the pavement, littered with nails.

"Good thing we didn't just bust through," I say.

Unsure of what to do, we edge closer to the barrier and gradually reach it. There's no one around and because there's no one around and it hasn't been raining, I don't think to shut the car doors. The car's still running, too. Wes and I examine the blockade and stare at the field of nails— hundreds, thousands. Someone doesn't want anyone to get through here, I think. I'm relieved I don't state the obvious aloud. We remain silent, and thus it's easier to hear the clicks and shouting behind us.

"Hands behind your head! Don't move!"

I look straight-ahead, afraid to make any sudden movements. Then I feel my arms being twisted behind my back and the cold wet metal of handcuffs.

"Turn around."

When I get a look at them, it's apparent they're a militia. The three in front of us are wearing camouflage fatigues, though their unkemptness and range of weapons (rifle, shotgun, handgun) makes them look more like a band of hunters than a quasi-military unit. The one on the right is chewing tobacco.

"We're Americans," I say, hoping to smooth over the situation. After I say it, I feel like an idiot.

"Not anymore you ain't," says the one in the middle. "Every man for himself now that everything's fucked up."

It takes restraint for me not to point out that he isn't exactly adhering to the "every man for himself" M.O. since he's part of a group. I wonder what they're going to do to us. Wes glances at me with an unsure look, and I'm thankful we're together at least.

"March. That way," the one with the rifle orders, pointing to his left with the gun. Wes and I gawk at the meager, barely noticeable path through the woods.

"What about the car?" I ask.

"Don't worry," says the middle one. "We'll take care of that. Jim, take 'em to the base." The one with the rifle and tobacco is Jim. He gets behind me and nudges me with his gun. We start walking toward the path and soon enter the woods. I'm reminded of my brief walk through the woods just a day earlier. It's more difficult to retain balance with my hands behind my back, and I'm hoping I won't fall. Even though questions shoot through my mind like arrows, I don't speak.

"So Jim," Wes says after a few minutes of walking, "where we headed?" Wes is in front of me, and Jim in back, but I'm still shocked he says anything. I'm afraid of getting shot, or worse. More unsettling is Jim's silence.

"This isn't the way it works in the movies, Erik. We're supposed to get captured by foreigners who don't speak English so we can talk about where they're taking us, and what they're gonna do, without them understanding."

Silence except for footsteps.

"Do you ever feel like a walking cliché, Jim? I would if I were you. Now, I haven't seen your teeth, but I bet they could use a good cleaning. Maybe even a sandblasting. How many heads do you have mounted on the walls of your trailer, Jim? A bunch, I'd say. As a matter of fact, I'd bet my left nut that your wardrobe is... What word am I looking for, Erik?"

"Consists of, most likely," I say to get him to keep the focus off me.

"Consists of. Exactly. Jim, I'd bet my left nut that your wardrobe consists of sleeveless T-shirts that have beer logos, eagles, racecars, and the American flag on them. And I'll have you know the man in front of you, Jim, is a general. A four-star general. Jim, have you ever made love to a general?"

I feel a sharp, sizzling pain in my back that makes me cringe, but I'm too shocked to cry out before Jim talks.

"Every time he talks, you get hit."

"Every time who talks?" Wes asks.

Jim hits me in the back again, forcing me to cry out.

"That sounded like a kidney shot, Erik."

Jim hits me again.

"Shut up, Wes," I say.

Following what could be a half an hour or more—Wes is quiet the rest of the way, thank God—the three of us reach a small clearing. There are several large tents. They circle a burnt-out campfire. Is this their headquarters? We stop upon reaching the entrance to what I presume is their base, or at least an outpost.

"Wait here. Don't move. It'll be worse if you do," Jim says. He then double-times it to one of the tents and slips inside.

"Let's get the fuck out of here," Wes whispers.

"That's a great idea. How long do you think it'd take for them to catch us? Two, three minutes?"

"You have a crush on Jim, don't you? I think he likes you, too."

"This is serious," still whispering. "We're handcuffed. We'd have to run. There's no way we can get out of this—not now."

Wes shrugs.

The tent opens and out marches a man, who I think must be the leader of the operation, with Jim in tow. He's wearing camouflage like the rest of them, but is bald and has silver aviator sunglasses on, which prevent me from seeing his eyes. He seems the epitome of a hardass, meaning we're in for a rough time.

"Ladies and gentlemen, I present to you Sergeant Stereotype," Wes says as they approach. Jim walks to me and jabs me in the stomach with his gun. I groan and fall to my knees, cursing Wes in my head, struggling to catch my breath.

Once the leader finishes looking both of us over—Jim assures him we're unarmed—he walks back in the direction of his tent.

"The Pit," he says, disappearing inside.

"Yes sir," Jim shouts. Addressing us, "Looks like you boys are headed to The Pit. Let's get going. To your right, now."

I figure Wes will ask Jim what The Pit is, but the question doesn't come. Either way, I know we'll find out what it is soon enough, and we make our way toward it by taking a short path—to the right of the camp—through the woods to another, smaller clearing. Due to the blazed yet subtle paths and the way the camp's organized, I believe this militia has been here for some time, that all this has been here long before the disasters.

Soon we converge at an empty pit with a wooden grate covering the hole. Not only does it look like it had to have been dug before any of these natural disasters occurred, but the few inches of standing muddy rainwater make it far less appealing, if that's even possible. Since we're still handcuffed and The Pit's not too deep—seven feet or so—I muster the courage to ask the question that first comes to mind: "Where are we supposed to go to the bathroom?"

Jim doesn't answer. Instead, he quickly pulls the covering to one side, which leaves the hole about half covered, and points to the open half.

"In," he says.

"Uh, in *there*?" Wes asks, out of disbelief. I don't want to believe it either.

"In," Jim repeats.

Wes is the first to make it down into the circular pit. I jump in next, awkwardly, and Jim pulls the grate over the rest of the hole, to its original position. The holes in the grate are big squares and we could reach them easily, except that our hands are handcuffed behind our backs. There's nothing we can do but stand in the muddy water. Jim's above us gazing down. He eventually tires of it and walks away.

"Well fuck," Wes says. "And here I thought the fucks were bluffing."

"They're more organized than I thought they'd be."

"So what do we do now, General?"

"Stand here, I guess, until you have to sit down."

"Why'd you ask the question about the bathroom? Isn't it obvious?"

"Of course it's obvious," I say, "but I was hoping we wouldn't have to resort to such barbarism."

"Now that you mention it, I gotta take a leak." A handcuffed Wes slides down the wall of The Pit until he's sitting. "It's like being in a tub of cold water. Let me see if I can warm it up."

I shake my head from side to side for a second, because I'm annoyed and disgusted. In fact, I move as far away from Wes as I can, but in such a small space, I can't move too much.

"Ah, that feels good," he says. "Too bad it's only warm for a minute."

"We'll probably get sick, especially if it rains again," I say, starting a different conversation. "They didn't even give us a chance to explain. I mean, what's the use of keeping us in here? It's not that we're a threat to them."

"Everyone's a threat now."

"Meaning?"

"We're all fighting for the same things—food, clothes, shelter. Now that everything's all fucked up, like that one guy said. Maybe it was just the Rapture and we're fucked anyway. Wouldn't that be nice? End of the world and stuff."

"Yes. And stuff."

"It's supposed to be warm tonight and the next few days, so we don't have to worry about freezing to death yet, even if we're wet."

"How do you know that?"

"I caught the ten-day forecast before the power went off. Supposed to be in the 60s all this week, but rainy. Fall's coming early this year. But you can never trust what they say, especially in this sort of situation."

"Sounds good," I say.

"Which part?"

"All of it. Some of it. None of it. I just don't see how it could get any worse, I guess."

"It'll be dark soon."

"Yeah. Do you think you'll be able to get any sleep tonight?"

"I can sleep anywhere at any time."

"Must be nice. I can't sleep sitting up. I have to be flat."

The rain arrives shortly after dark, pounding us and the pool we're partially submerged in. The grate provides no shelter from the downpour. It's too loud to talk without shouting, so I allow my thoughts to drift. Every time a family member enters my mind, I throw the thought out of my head but it always returns, like a boomerang. I think of Mom baking cookies, Dad reading in his study, Josh frowning while watching TV, and Jamie dragging Oink around the house, accidentally dropping him in the toilet but calling it "giving Oink a bath."

Since my friends were at home or close to home when the disasters struck, I'm more optimistic about their fates and find it easier to think about them without getting depressed. Still, my thoughts revert to what lies before me—a watery cell, a death by drowning sentence being carried out slowly but surely. I try to imagine what it would feel like to drown. I can't. I've heard you vomit first, but I don't see how that's possible. Somehow, I fall asleep.

The cave is dark, but I have no problem navigating without a flashlight. I've been temporarily outfitted with night-vision goggles, or something to that effect, but my vision isn't green. It's normal.

I've always liked the sounds of caves. Even at their quietest—with the dripping water, occasional stream, and echoes—caves are loud. I notice my surroundings more at this point, taking my time while observing the stalactites and stalagmites. The dripping water, which forms such things, reminds me of a leaky faucet, but in this sort of environment it doesn't bother me. I repress the need to quell the sound, as if there's a knob I could turn.

Around the bend, the ceilings jump from seven or eight feet high to twice that, if not more. I'm on higher ground than the cavern in front of me, and in looking for a way to get to the lower level, I notice the ladder. It's as if someone knows I'm coming. I expect my vision to falter, but it never does. Were my eyes made to function better at night than in the daytime? The ladder proves sturdy, so it's easy to make it to the floor. There's another turn at the far end of the cavern, and my stomach knots when I realize why I'm here and what might happen.

"So you've made it," says the mother kitten, atop a chair. She's on a panel. There's a banner in front of the table. It looks like this:

# SALVATION THROUGH FEAR

"That banner," I say, "is interesting. It looks uneven."

"No one's perfect." I remember the voice of Jesus, who's sitting on the very left with His halo shining brilliantly. "Well," He says, realizing the irony in His statement, "you know what I mean."

Between Christ and the mother kitten is the horse—another recurring, enigmatic figure—and to the right of the mother kitten is Wes, who appears dead.

"You've noticed your dead friend then, huh? Don't worry about him," Jesus says. "You know what?" I say. "I don't like You. And he's not my friend."

"Oh really?!" Jesus asks, feigning shock. "You've never liked Me! Whether you've actually taken the time to say it, and said it aloud doesn't matter—I've known. In fact, I've known for quite some time."

"What's Wes doing up there?"

He's leaning back in his chair with his mouth open, as if he fell asleep in the position. His hair hangs like it's frozen.

"He's fine. Really, he is," says the mother kitten who's obviously trying to console me. Her tail's wagging to and fro, I notice, as it always is when we're together. "Now, the point of this meeting is—"

"Dancing," Jesus interrupts. "Dancing. We must dance." Without any of them getting up from their spots, a number of strobe lights—whose locations are unknown to me—come to life and drown the cavern in slow-motion glory. My eyes don't react to the sudden influx of bright light.

"Where's the music?" I ask. Immediately after the question escapes my lips, techno starts blaring from an unidentifiable source, and the only words I decipher are "Making love," doctored to sound robotic. The beat and corresponding lyrics repeat with no end in sight.

I've got to get the fuck outta here.

"So use the bathroom!" Jesus shouts above the noise.

I notice the door to my left and walk to it in slo-mo. As I pass through, I feel weightless—like I could jump and simply float away, until I bang my head on the ceiling. Thankfully the music stays on the other side of the door, though the pounding continues relentlessly. For a moment, it's as if I'm at a club and will eventually return to the chaos, of which alcohol is the catalyst or one of many contributors.

The bathroom floor has a black and white checkered pattern. There's an empty stall directly across from the door, two urinals, and a sink to the right. To my surprise, there's already some guy pissing at one of the urinals, so when I belly up to mine, I look him in the eye and nod. With his dirt-caked complexion, ratty long hair, and tattered, holey trench coat, he resembles a bum. I stare straight at the black wall in front of me and concentrate on the muffled techno beat.

"I got saved when I was six," he says, like he's resuming a conversation. "Out of fear, mostly. I was afraid. Afraid of Hell. The description—fire, brimstone, pain—is terrifying." I think he'll keep talking, but he doesn't.

"That's not how it's supposed to work, though, is it?" I ask, suddenly feeling outgoing, brave. "When I used to go to church, everyone told me you're supposed to get saved because you love God, because you know you've sinned and you want forgiveness for your sins. I can't picture it working the other way. It just seems..."

The pounding stops. The bathroom gives way to complete darkness. In an instant, I'm in a church. I'm in a pew facing the bum, who is now dressed as a priest and behind the podium holding the Bible in the air. We're in a cathedral.

"Self-centered? Yes! Yes you are! All of us want to preserve ourselves. None of us can get away from that urge, that desire to do what's in our best interest so we can continue living, this notion of self-preservation. Some say 'God helps those who help themselves,' but rest assured you won't find that in here." He slaps the Bible with an open palm. "I've been saved more times than I can remember — not that any of them count. You are either saved or you aren't, and though I would ask and believe I was saved, I would always fall back in the same rut. Deep down, I knew I just wasn't meant to be in that group of people who call themselves Christians and mean it. For some time, I found it easier to believe in Hell than in God. God is so *abstract*. The concepts fly above our heads, and we can't even begin to grasp them. Can you fathom a being who wasn't created, but who's always existed? Can you truly understand omnipresence? Can you imagine what eternity is like?"

I think: No, not at all. When I think about any of those things, I know it's beyond my ability. Feeling brave again, I say, "So what do you believe about God?"

"It doesn't matter! I look around and see these things in nature — some call it Creationism, others call it Intelligent Design, and yet others call it evolution — and can't help but think there's a higher power who created all this. Did a being set everything into motion? How could the planet, the galaxy, the universe, the multiverse, be a product of mere chance? A result derived from nothing? Everything is more complex than it seems."

"What about God? What do you think about Him?" I ask.

"It doesn't matter. Now remove your outer garments so that I may baptize your penis in the waters of my mouth."

"What the fuck?" I say, getting out of the pew. I backpedal toward the cathedral's entrance, and on the way, realize I'm naked.

"Come back here!" the priest says.

"You're playing into the stereotype. You can live for yourself, make your own mark. Leave your own legacy for the good of society."

The pounding begins. The cathedral gives way to complete darkness. In an instant, I'm in the bathroom. I'm at the urinal next to the bum, who is now dressed as a bum again.

"You have to figure that out for yourself," he says. "I can't help you there, but I'll tell ya, I wouldn't want to be in your shoes, even though they're nice. Top of the line Nikes. Very nice. You've got a rough road ahead of you, so good luck."

"Thanks. I won't even bother asking what you're talking about, but how am I supposed to get out of here? I mean out of the cave."

"Go through that door to your left," he says, looking at me but pointing to the wall to my left.

"Oh, I didn't even see it, with it being black and all."

"Good luck," he says as he resumes staring in front of him.

"Thanks," I say. "You, too." It's a slide door with no doorknob, so I slide it open and step into total darkness. I hear voices in the distance and the sliding of the wooden grate. My eyes slowly adjust to the light.

# CHAPTER FOUR:
# ERIK & WES MEET JENNA

They're throwing a chick in here," Wes says.

I look at him, and then up at Jim who's behind the girl about to be tossed into The Pit. Her hands, like ours, are behind her back, and even though I can't see them, I know they're handcuffed. I wonder where she came from and where she was headed before the militia captured her.

Jim pushes her forward and she falls awkwardly into The Pit. The muddy splash sprays Wes and me. The rainwater's accumulated for who knows how long, but it's not a threat to any of us—just an annoyance. The standing water makes it much more difficult to sleep, too. I haven't had to crap in the water yet, and I'm dreading the moment I do. It'll be like wearing a wet diaper.

What's more, Wes's cough has increased in frequency, and sounds worse as time passes. It's gruff and wet—it sounds like he needs to get rid of mucous. Occasionally he'll have a coughing fit that he'll have to bear until it subsides. When this happens, he leans forward and coughs toward the water. If he has to spit, he spits in the water. I cringe at the thought of more bodily fluids floating in the pool. I told him to cover his mouth once—a bad joke—but he just shrugged.

After she arranges herself against the side—opposite me and Wes—she looks each of us over. The first thing I ask myself, as usual, is, Would I have sex with her? I answer: Yes. Wes's presence leads to another question, though, which is, Who is she more likely to have sex with—Wes or me? I answer: I don't know. Wes has the physical edge and maybe the charm, too, but I'm more intelligent and probably have a better personality. There's also personal preference—the unpredictable "it" factor that could screw me.

Jim stands like he did when he threw us in. For several minutes he just glares, I assume due to his aviator shades, and after a while, he slides the grate over the hole and walks off.

"Come here often?" Wes asks the girl.

"No," she says. I study her more closely. She has a slender, if ordinary, body and is wearing jeans and a sweater. Her long black hair is pulled into a ponytail, and though her face is pale, her lips are full. She's definitely attractive and I find myself comparing her and Mandy—my former next-door neighbor. I wonder where *she* is. I can't decide on a winner, and given the opportunity, I would have sex with both—preferably at the same time.

"What do you think they're gonna do to us?" I ask.

"Obviously they're capturing anyone that uses the Interstate," she says in a Southern drawl. "My name's Jenna."

"I'm Wes. He's Erik, but I call him the General because he likes it."

"I don't like it, but I *am* Erik. Good to meet you."

"How long have you guys been in here?"

"Since yesterday," Wes says.

"How are your feet doing?" she asks.

"Fine. Why?" I ask.

"If your feet are wet for a long time, they'll get blisters. It'll get worse if the conditions persist. I learned about it in my World War I history class."

"Damn," Wes says. "I'm doing all right so far."

"Me too, but I'll keep that in mind," I say. "Where were you headed?" She launches into a story about how she goes to school a little ways north from us—she's originally from Louisiana—but is also headed south in hopes of meeting up with her parents since she couldn't reach them by phone or e-mail before she left.

"NOLA then, huh?" I ask.

"Yep. NOLA," she says.

"NOLA?" Wes asks, turning to me for an explanation, causing ripples with his movement.

"Yeah, NOLA," I say, "N O for New Orleans and L A for Louisiana."

"Okay," he says.

"Man," I say, as if coming to a realization, "I'm hungry."

"Me too," Wes says.

"Me three. And where are we supposed to use the bathroom?" Jenna says.

"You're looking at it," Wes says.

"Oh," she says.

"It's not so bad," he says. "Piss feels nice and warm for a minute."

"It *is* so bad," I say.

"How long's it been since we ate?" Wes asks me.

"I don't know. I guess, uh—"

"What, twelve hours?"

"Maybe. I have no idea."

"What do you think they'll bring us?" asks Jenna. "They have to feed us, right?"

"Yeah," I say. If my arms were free, I would bring a hand to my face, in an attempt to look like I'm mulling over the situation. "They've got to," I continue, "if they don't want us to die. I'm sure they'll bring us water and food and stuff." I'm trying to lighten the mood by feigning optimism—not so much for myself as for Wes and Jenna. "Knock on wood."

"I bet we can get that off somehow," Wes says, gazing upward at the wooden grate.

"How?" Jenna asks. In thinking about it, however, I zone out on the conversation for a minute or two.

"—and then all we have to do is get the cuffs off," he says.

"What was that?" I ask.

"We basically just have to lure a guard down in here and then knock him out," he says, "then take the keys off him and unlock each other."

"I don't think that'll work, man. I mean, even one of those guys probably wouldn't fall for that."

"You got a better idea then?" Wes asks, repeating a question I asked him yesterday. I remain silent for a moment, as if I'm thinking about which of my many, great plans is the best.

"No. No, I don't."

"So we're gonna go along with this? Cuz if we are, we should start figuring out how the fuck we're gonna do it."

"I guess I—"

"Wait," Jenna says. We both turn to look at her. "Have you tried getting the cuffs off?"

"We can't," I say. "They're behind our backs. I'm not that flexible."

"I don't like telling people this—especially guys and especially when I don't know them too well—but I'm really flexible. I think I can get out of these handcuffs," she says.

"Nice," Wes says.

Shouts sound off from the other clearing, triggering our silence. A few minutes later, Jim approaches the hole and looks at us. It's an image that, because of its frequency and my helplessness, will remain with me forever. I hope it won't, but I think it will. His hands are down at his sides, but I can tell he has a few PowerBars, our PowerBars, in one of them. I try to count exactly how many he's holding—how many, in turn, each of us will get. Despite my best efforts, I can't tell.

"Food," Jim says, sluggishly tossing the PowerBars onto the wooden grate. Each lands with a splash, except for one, which gets stuck on the grate where four beams intersect. Jim hunches down, presumably to nudge it off and send it airborne to plummet into the murky pool, but thinks better of it, returning to an upright position. He smirks at us, though we can't see his eyes or tell who he's looking at exactly thanks to his reflective lenses. Then, without saying another word, he turns and walks toward camp.

"That son of a bitch," Wes says.

"Yeah," I agree without a trace of emotion.

It's difficult locating the PowerBars in the opaque water—especially with our hands behind our backs. We get on our knees and sift through the pool as if searching for gold. The finds are just as exhilarating. It's equally difficult to eat. One person opens a PowerBar, turns around, and lets another eat out of his/her hands. It's by far the strangest and most drawn-out meal I've ever had.

There are five bars to go around, but that excludes the one resting atop the grate, which I imagine will drop sooner or later. We save one of the bars because we figure we'll need it, if they decide not to feed us again. A little later, however, Jim returns to The Pit carrying a white grocery sack. He removes one plastic bottle of water at a time, casually lobbing them in the air. One by one they fall into the pool. On the way down, the last bottle hits the suspended PowerBar, knocking it through one of the square holes before it crashes into the water below. Our stockpile increases from one to two.

After gulping down enough water to sate our thirsts—again, the same painstaking process is used to open the bottles and drink—we have the better part of the day to hatch our escape plan.

"So you're saying you can get out of those cuffs?" I ask Jenna.

"No, all I'm saying is that I can get my hands in front of me."

"I used to pick locks," Wes says. "My dad showed me how to pick a few different types, and with one of the hairpins you have on, Jenna," he says, "I could probably do it."

"Looks like I'm the diversion, huh?" I ask. I hope they won't take me up on my sarcastic offer. Before anyone can jump in, I say, "We'll want to leave right after lunch—right after Jim brings us food tomorrow. There's no way we'll be able to navigate the woods at night. It'll be colder then, too." I notice Jenna doesn't have a jacket or coat or anything.

"You're right," says Jenna.

"Yes—" says Wes, who then coughs repeatedly.

"You sound bad, man," I say.

"I told you I'm getting sick."

"But yeah, I think once it's daylight tomorrow we should start getting ready to leave. We'll of course have to act like we're still handcuffed when Jim comes around. Let's just hope they don't decide to do anything with us tonight or tomorrow morning."

"What'll we do once we get out? And how're we gonna get out of here?" Jenna asks.

"Well," I say, "I figure I can stand on Wes's back to remove the grate—I'll just slide it to one side—and then climb outta here, hoist you up, and then we'll both hafta help Wes up. You'll have to get our handcuffs off first, though."

"Where are we gonna go?" Jenna asks.

"I don't know, but I think our best bet is to head in the opposite direction of the camp—there's bound to be a trail leading out of here. Eventually I think we should head to the Interstate."

"Why?" asks Wes.

"Shelter. Food. Maybe we'll run into someone who can help us. Besides, we won't last too long in these woods, if it gets a lot colder. Plus, Jenna doesn't have a jacket on either."

"What if it rains tomorrow? We'll be fucked," Wes says.

"Yeah, if it rains tomorrow, then we'll just have to stay here till it stops, and till it's daytime again."

"It sounds like it might work," Jenna says. Her comments give me an added sense of confidence, even though I think my plan is logical and better than anything else we come up with. It's certainly better than Wes's *Three Stooges*-type plan.

"Let's hope it does," I say and then lean my head back and shut my eyes.

I can't sleep, but as I relax, my thoughts transport me elsewhere. For some reason I recall a fall afternoon, long ago, when I was in the backyard playing. This was at our old house, the one we lived in before we moved to Pleasant Hills. I'd just gotten home from the toy store where my parents bought me a big red ball. It was half as tall as I was, and bouncy. Though I knew it'd get stuck in one of the colossal trees in our backyard if I continued kicking it high in the air, I still did.

Eventually it got stuck. I wasn't surprised, but I was still disappointed. I'd just gotten it, and it was stuck too high to do anything about it. As the seasons changed, it lost air and its bright red sheen faded as the weather took its toll. During a summer day or night the following year it tumbled from its perch and I found it soon afterward, deflated. I didn't even want the thing anymore. By that time I'd transitioned from aimless games to soccer. There was an objective, plus the ball was too heavy to kick very high, but too small to get lodged in the branches of one of our trees. I took the remains of the big red ball in my hands and tossed it in the trash, or maybe I tried to kick it in there—kick it one last time.

Wes and Jenna continue to talk, but I'm not in the mood so I do my best to tune them out. They're talking about college or whatever. I don't care. Suddenly I'm in a foul mood, probably due to all the circumstances I've been forced to endure recently—the rain, The Pit, lack of food, having to piss and crap in the same place we're all confined to, the list goes on. I haven't taken a crap yet, but I haven't ever been constipated, so I'm expecting the inevitable to occur soon.

I visualize a screensaver I've seen on a countless number of computers. I'm traveling through space—I don't think about what I'm in or how I'm able to do this—passing millions of stars that look like small, perfectly round snowflakes. This brings questions to mind. Is there a God? Yes, no, maybe. I'm not sure. I feel as if I can't be sure, like I won't ever be sure. I've heard the arguments from many perspectives, but a few opposing viewpoints make sense to me. I can't decide. What's the point of deciding anyway? I can't answer that question either.

Then I think about my yard again, and how we used to have this dog—we went through lots of dogs—that used to lie on our only yucca plant. As a result of such activity, he flattened it so that the leaves looked like they were growing toward the ground. He was destructive, which was why we gave him to another family. I think they owned a farm, and everyone figured he needed a wide-open space with plenty of room to roam. I always wondered how the other animals reacted to him.

Besides one of the dogs we had, I never got too attached to a pet until we got the cats. Our personalities are more alike. They can occupy themselves, for the most part, and enjoy life by sleeping through most of it. I heard, somewhere, that cats sleep fourteen hours a day, but when I tried to replicate such behavior on several occasions, I'd get a headache. Fur would be good, too, at least in the situation I'm in. I'd be warmer, I bet. So I'd take a cat's schedule, fur, superior sense of smelling and hearing, but I'd keep my brain so I wouldn't be dumb, even though cats are smart for animals. I picture how big a cat's head would have to be for my brain to fit inside and it's incredibly disproportionate to its body. I can't help but laugh at the imagery. I can't help but laugh out loud.

"What's so funny?" Wes asks, a confused look on his face.

"Nothing, man," I say, trying to avoid the subject because I don't want to explain. There isn't much else to do but talk, so that's what we do. We talk about the plan, mostly, continually running it over the way it's supposed to pan out, the way we hope it will.

Before night falls we each eat a couple bites of our second to last PowerBar, killing it, and drink gulps of water, which is supposed to tide us over for the night. Once the darkness descends, it's too difficult to see—at least enough not to bother trying to eat and drink in handcuffs. I'm tired of having my hands behind my back. In fact, I'm tired of a lot of things. I'm uncomfortable and sore. My feet are starting to ache. At first I was afraid to leave The Pit at the thought of them doing something terrible to me, but now I think leaving The Pit would be a relief no matter what they do. Still, even while sitting in the dirty water, I'm able to get some sleep.

The sunlight's blinding, but I still feel the uncontrollable urge to open my eyes while spitting and coughing out the sand I've somehow gotten in my mouth. It's as dry as a mouthful of salt, and when I chomp on the grains, it's gritty and loud like the sound of tiny fireworks. After ridding my mouth of what sand I can, I stand up, from all fours, and look at the horizon. There are dunes everywhere, which stretch out as far as I can see, and I know I'm smack dab in the middle of a desert.

"You look like shit!" yells a voice from behind. I feel a sense of alarm and beads of sweat forming on my brow.

"Jesus Christ," I say, turning around. He's a few feet away from me. I want to describe His appearance, and though the words reverberate in my head like pinballs, I can't utter a single detail, a single attribute.

"Well, yeah," He says. Then He kicks sand in my direction, but nonchalantly, like He's playing around.

"What's all this?" I ask, motioning to the endless desert.

"This, my friend, is the wide world of creation, and it looks like you're gonna walk it."

"Great. I've had my fill of walking. I get thirsty just thinking about it. What about You, though? Aren't You gonna walk with me? Once I collapse aren't You supposed to carry me, leaving only one set of footprints when originally there were two?"

"Yes and no."

"What do You mean by that?"

"I'll show you when you start walking."

"Fine." I turn back around and trudge in a random direction. Sand's consistency is kind of like snow's—they both slow you down considerably. To my left, Jesus is sitting Indian-style, or Native American-style, I guess, and floating like a genie accompanying his master, or an Arab sitting atop a flying carpet. "Nice," I tell Him.

"I like it."

"So listen, where are We going?"

"How should I know? You're the one leading."

"Yeah, but You're the one who's supposed to know everything—omniscience, or whatever. And hey, aren't We not on the best of terms?"

"I'm not mad if you're not mad. And yes, I do know everything, but that doesn't mean I should reveal anything to you. Why should I? Do you think you're entitled to know everything you wanna know?"

"No, I guess not, but it'd be cool, You know, for You to, like, reveal stuff. That way I don't have to wonder so much."

"Now We're talking about more than where We're headed aren't We? Imagine every grain of sand you see is one piece of knowledge. You know less than a handful. In fact, you know merely a speck. A speck with camel piss all over it."

"This is a parable then?"

"Yeah," He scoffs, "as if I have nothing better to do than fling parables at everyone all the time. Screw that."

The sand's hot on my feet and is sticking to me like Velcro.

"You would appreciate the extreme heat if subjected to extreme cold for even one second."

"You're prolly right. It's like that Robert Frost poem 'Fire and Ice.'"

"Robert Frost is a queer," He says.

"Is he?"

"I don't know. If he's in Heaven, I'll ask him. If he's in Hell, I'll get Satan to. By the way, this dream's about over."

"What? Why? I haven't gotten anywhere! There are just dunes everywhere—no oasis."

"Things are sometimes not what they seem."

"I know that."

"Besides," He says, "here comes your friend." I look to my right, in the direction He pointed, and there, not too far off, is that white horse moping toward me. "It'll take him a while to get here, especially if you keep walking, but you're not supposed to meet him yet. At least I don't think so."

"Why's he keep appearing? What's he symbolize?" I ask, gazing in the horse's direction. When I turn to look at Jesus, there's no one there.

W ake up," Wes says. And then I hear a tiny splash and feel drops of water hit my face.

"I'm awake."

"It's morning, Erik," says Jenna.

"Congratulations," I say.

"So the plan then, huh?" asks Wes.

"Yeah, the plan. Once Jim delivers our meal," I say, "we'll head out. I'm hungry now, though. Anyone else wanna eat?"

I feel disgusting having not showered for days. How much money would it take for me to drink some of The

Pit's water? No amount sounds big enough. The knee-high standing water keeps us in a constant, chilled state and prevents restful sleep. My feet are starting to swell, I think, which will hinder my escape. Nevertheless, I can't shake my hunger despite the sickening conditions.

"I could use a bite," Wes says.

"Me, too," Jenna says.

"Let's get started then."

We don't know when Jim will appear, so we don't take any stupid chances like trying to pick our handcuffs. We eat the last of our stockpile—a PowerBar and some water—the way we pioneered earlier. One person eats out of another's hands whose back is turned. Like last time, it takes forever for all three of us to eat and drink.

Soon after we finish, Jim's above us with the wooden grate partially obscuring our view of him. He has another guy with him—a prisoner, who, like us, has his hands handcuffed behind his back. This guy's short, fat, and dressed in a black hoodie, black jeans, and black shoes. He's got a pudgy face and short, straight black hair. Looks like he's trying to grow a beard, but it's the patchiest one I've ever seen. I notice Jim's aviator shades again, and begin to think he never takes them off, even when he sleeps. He slides the grate to one side. Then he positions himself behind the kid, and with more force than necessary, kicks him toward The Pit, which sends him flying into it. He lands with a splash and muffled thud, narrowly missing our legs. Since he couldn't brace himself with his hands or arms, his face becomes submerged in the murky, shitty water, and when he's upright, he spits out the water that entered his mouth.

Jim throws more PowerBars and bottles of water into The Pit, and like before, we have to pan the water to retrieve them.

"Breakfast, bitches," Jim says. He bends down and places the grate over the hole. He walks to camp afterward.

"What's your name?" Wes asks when Jim is gone.

"Brad."

"Brad, we're getting outta here so you can either come with us or stay here."

"Who made you leader?"

"What'd you say?" Wes asks.

"You heard me," Brad says.

"Listen, kid. You're lucky I'm handcuffed right now or I'd slap some sense into you."

"All right," I interrupt, "let's get going."

All we can do while Jenna contorts her body to get her hands in front of her is stare in awe and disbelief. Though a lot of guys find flexibility sexy, I've never understood the appeal. Still, I have to admit it's practical in this situation. When she finishes, she reaches up, removes the bobby pin from her hair, and hands it to Wes.

Wes's job is perhaps the most difficult because he tells us he has to fold the bobby pin into the right shape and pick the handcuff lock—all behind his back. I'm hoping the handcuffs aren't double-locked, because that'd add an extra step to an already difficult process. One time I watched an Internet video about how to unlock handcuffs with a bobby pin, but I didn't think I'd be able to duplicate the video's results like Wes, a semi-professional, can, so I'm glad he's here. At the moment, I wonder if I'll ever not want him around.

It takes several minutes because he's essentially working blindly, though once his hands are free, he has each of us out in no time. "Got 'em," he says as he unlatches the cuffs and drops them into the dirty water. Of course, as I silently predicted, he unlocks Jenna next. I harbor a little resentment. Why is it that guys turn everything into a contest with a clear winner and a clear loser?

It's great to stretch, and for the first time in days, move freely.

"Wow," I say, "screw those things!"

"So how're we getting out of here?" Brad asks.

"You'll go second," I say.

"What?"

"Just watch."

Since The Pit is deep and the mud is slick, due to the intermittent rain, Wes and Jenna kneel as if practicing a tornado drill and I stand on their backs—one foot on Wes's and one on Jenna's—while I slide the grate to one side. It's heavy, but I manage. I jump up the side and dig my fingers into the moist dirt and slowly pull myself up. I stay low to the ground and look around. The coast is clear—no Jim, or anyone else for that matter.

Brad's next because he'd be too heavy for the rest of us to pull out, plus if he goes last, he might not make it out if Wes and Jenna don't push him from below. Thus, Brad follows my lead, climbing on top of Wes and Jenna in order to jump out. After his boost, I grab one of his arms and pull him out. Jenna goes after that. She steadies herself on Wes's back while I help her up. Brad's just standing around. Wes is last. Jenna scrutinizes the surroundings but says she doesn't see anything. That's about as good as it could go. When we're all out, I place the grate over The Pit.

"It'll give us more time," I say in explanation, knowing an open hole will be discovered sooner than a closed one.

"Let's get outta here," Wes whispers. And then we're jogging into the woods, despite our weakened muscles and feet, in the opposite direction of the camp.

Shit," says Wes, who's in front. We're a couple hundred feet into the woods and we stop when he speaks up.

"What?" I ask.

"We left all that shit back there."

"What shit?"

"The PowerBars and water."

"We've gotta go back," says Jenna.

"I don't think we should," I say. "It's too risky. We got out once. If they catch us again, there's no telling what they'll do."

"Right," Wes says.

"We've gotta keep moving and hope we find provisions along the way, or at least where we end up for the night."

"What if they have dogs?" Brad asks to no one in particular.

"Dogs?" Wes asks.

"Are you stupid?" Brad says.

"You mean, like, bloodhounds or German shepherds?" I ask.

"Yeah," Brad says.

"Then we're screwed."

We set off again, deeper into the woods despite the absence of a trail. I'm tired immediately. I haven't jogged in a week, and after being scrunched up in The Pit, my body's uncooperative. I have no idea which direction we're going, or what we'll potentially stumble on. Luckily, I remember that as long as we continue walking straight ahead, and don't veer too much, we're still parallel to the Interstate—for a few miles. There's also the fact that it's only a matter of time until the militia discovers our escape. Then the manhunt will begin. Or, due to the shortage of gas and the inability to procure it, maybe they'll intentionally forget about us. Maybe Jim'll be punished for letting us get away. The thought puts a smile on my face.

Quickly I lose track of how much ground we've covered, and while Wes, Jenna, and me are able to keep pace with one another—albeit a slow pace—each time we stop to rest, Brad's farther behind.

"What are you guys?" Brad asks between pants, when he isn't gasping for air, "fucking long-distance runners?"

"You're just fat and slow," Wes says. He stares at Brad, knowing he'll do nothing. I've sensed a change in Wes ever since Brad arrived. Brad bends over and places his hands on his knees, trying to catch his breath.

"Go fuck yourself," Brad says.

"Quit arguing," I say, looking more at Wes than Brad.

"Okay," Wes says. He situates his hair behind his ears so it'll be out of his face momentarily. Still, there's no way to keep his long, curly brown hair out of his face for too long, especially when running, unless he ties it behind his head. It's at this point that I know Wes and Brad are destined to clash. While Wes is slender, average-looking, and sometimes assertive, Brad is fat, ugly, and always assertive. It seems they're on opposite ends of the human spectrum.

For a second I think in Darwinian terms. In a survival of the fittest scenario, which we're sort of in, Wes is the superior specimen and will most likely come out on top.

"Let's keep going," Wes says.

"Sounds good," I say. As a result of lack of proper food and no water, the pace gradually devolves from sprinting to jogging to trudging. The longer we exert effort and energy, the deeper we get into the woods.

"Need another break," Brad shouts from behind again.

"Dammit!" I hear Wes yell from in front. During the breather, Jenna sits against a tree, Wes paces, Brad leans over like before, and I stand still. I'm picking the skin off my thumbs again—a nervous habit I've had ever since I could remember. I've seen other people tear the skin from their other fingers, but not just their thumbs. I wonder if there's a name for the habit.

"By the way," Wes says, "don't fucking yell shit." He's talking to Brad. "We're trying to escape here—not get captured again, idiot." Brad remains silent for once, but rolls his eyes.

I know there's trouble as soon as Wes stomps toward Brad with a determined look in his eyes and balled-up fists—prominent blue veins running down his arms like vines. Brad and Wes are nose to nose with each other.

"Hey," Brad says casually.

I laugh. Here's a confrontation about to explode under horrible conditions and Brad's taking everything in stride, or backing down from a fight he knows he'll lose. They look at me, and then, before any of us can say or do anything, Wes sucker punches Brad in the face. Brad's nose is probably broken—judging by the amount of blood—but he won't realize it until much later because he's out before he hits the ground.

I'm in shock, but I glance at Jenna who looks away after our eyes meet. Someone has to address what Wes has done—someone has to say *something*. I look at Wes.

"He'll only slow us down in the long run," he says, explaining himself. "Besides, we'll have more time if they find him before us. We'll have more time to get away from here."

"You mean...you think we should leave him?" I ask.

"Exactly," Wes says.

"Dude, we can't."

"I'm going to." Wes turns and walks farther into the woods. It begins to rain large drops that drench us while we consider our options.

"We can't just leave him," I tell Jenna, who's still sitting.

I lean down next to Brad and tap his cheek with my finger, careful to avoid the blood. The rain doesn't wake him either, so he's officially out. I turn toward Wes. His back's still in view, shrinking by the minute as blazes a path that remains undetectable in defiance of his efforts. When he's out of sight, we won't be able to follow him even if we want to.

"I know," says Jenna, "but we might have to."

"I don't wanna leave him here, but I don't want The Pit again. He's too heavy to carry. No telling how long he'll be out. I'm sure he'll be all right when he comes to. And we don't know if they even know we're gone yet."

"Right."

"Let's just go then, I guess. I hate to, but there's no other option. Let's head toward the Interstate so we can see where we are, plus it'll be easier to cover ground, and quicker since there are ditches we can walk in."

"Fine."

Jenna gets to her feet. As we head off in a perpendicular direction from Wes and the incapacitated Brad, we have to shout to hear each other because the rain is so loud.

"I'm kind of glad Wes is gone," I whisper, wanting to say it aloud without her hearing. "Something wasn't right with him."

We make our way through the woods—me in front, Jenna following—and the rain eases, although not completely. Still, it's light enough that we can talk without having to shout.

"It just occurred to me that this is, like, *Lord of the Flies*. Did you ever read that?" I ask.

"No," she says, "but I remember watching part of the movie on TV."

"Yeah, it's like Wes is turning into Jack, Brad is Piggy, and I'm Ralph."

"Who does that make me?"

"What?"

"Who am I? If we're all characters from the book, then who am I?"

"Nobody, I guess." I regret my diction immediately. "I mean, you're not nobody. You're just not, uh, well, there weren't any females on the island, so…"

"How far to the Interstate?" she asks. I'm grateful for the intentional change of subject.

"I don't really know. We were parallel to it when we were in The Pit, so heading in the same direction and then turning like we did should put us there pretty soon. Maybe we're not going in the right direction. I don't know. We'll see. My feet are killing me. I can't wait to change into dry clothes."

"Me too."

The rain continues, soaking us because we've been in it a long time. The woods are thick, though, and the canopy shields us from some of the downpour. While it keeps us colder and wetter than I'd prefer, it also helps wash off the mud and dirt and crap that got on us in The Pit. I'm desperate for a hot shower and a hot meal—in that order—but I doubt I'll ever partake of either again.

"What happens when we find the Interstate?" Jenna asks.

"Just follow it, I guess."

"That's the plan?"

"Looks like it. Do you have a better idea?"

"No."

"I don't mean to jinx us by throwing a best case scenario out there, but hopefully we'll find the Interstate and somewhere covered to sleep before it's dark. Let's hope we find Wes and Brad, and hope that Wes has come to his senses," I say, pushing small branches out of the way.

"Maybe it's better if we don't run into them. Certain people just don't get along with each other. I knew tons of people in high school who would make fun of kids like Brad for being overweight. Some people just don't get along even if they try to—not saying that Wes was trying to. He obviously overreacted."

"I know what you mean. I hadn't had a problem with Wes at all, and I still don't, but he seems to be acting differently lately. He might think he'll be better off without us and needed a reason to ditch. I dunno. We might find out."

We continue plowing through the woods, anticipating the sight of paved concrete. Later, I, in the front, catch a glimpse of gray peeking through the overgrowth. The rain has practically stopped, probably not for long.

"I think that's it!" I say to Jenna, halfway excited. "I think we made it finally."

"Good." Evidently she hasn't grasped the gravity of the situation, of our discovery. Once we reach the tree line, where construction workers cleared the land to make a path for the Interstate however many decades ago, we stand looking at a barren stretch of road, save for what appears to be a car in the ditch quite a ways ahead. It's too early to tell if we'll be able to use it for anything.

"Which direction do you think we should go?" Jenna asks.

"Me and Wes were going that way," I say, pointing in the direction of the car, which is northbound, "but we didn't get this far before we got captured."

"Where do you think he is now?"

"I dunno, but if we head the opposite direction, we'll be heading toward that militia's camp."

"You think they've recaptured Wes or Brad yet?"

"I doubt they'd bother, unless it's a pride thing, in which case they'd try."

"They might not stop looking until they've captured us again—all of us."

"Maybe. It's prolly one or the other. Oh well. Screw it," I say, then shrug. "We might as well start walking. Hopefully we'll run into something soon. We'll check out that car, too."

"Fine."

There's not much of a point in sticking to the ditch. If they're gonna catch us, they're gonna catch us. If someone's gonna find us, someone's gonna find us. I'm tired of walking on ground anyway.

"It's weird that we haven't seen anybody yet," she says.

"Yeah, it's like everyone dropped off the face of the Earth. Maybe it's the Rapture. I'm sure we'll run into Wes or somebody else soon enough."

"Let's check out that car up there."

"Sure. We should."

It's a maroon Ford Taurus and both the driver's side and passenger's side doors are open as if the car was abandoned in haste, as if the occupants were yanked from it against their will. The interior's pretty clean, however, and while the outside's dirty, it isn't damaged.

"I guess we'd be asking for too much if we prayed for it to start," Jenna says.

"Prayer doesn't work," I say, "but you can try if you want. Besides," I say, feeling for the keys in the ignition, "the keys are gone." I reach beside the driver's seat and pop the hood so I can take a useless gander at the car's innards.

"Why did I even bother?" I ask myself. "I don't know anything about cars—much less how to hotwire one." I shut the hood.

Jenna, who's next to me with her arms crossed and peering under the hood too, says, "I don't either."

"Let's check the trunk for anything we might be able to use." When I'm opening the trunk, after popping it of course, I expect to find a dead body, or someone bound and gagged, but it proves empty except for a tire iron, which I immediately grab, relishing the power of crafted iron in my hand. If needed, it's capable of inflicting major damage.

"Can use this maybe," I say. Jenna just nods. "Cold?"

"Yeah."

"Maybe we'll find a gas station soon," I say, shutting the trunk. Then, like someone suffering from OCD, I shut the driver's side door, walk around the front of the car, and shut the passenger's side. It'll bother me too much if I leave them open.

"I know—I'm weird," I tell her.

"I'd probly do it, too."

Holding the tire iron in my right hand, I resume walking.

# CHAPTER FIVE:
# ERIK & JENNA HEAD EAST

It's good to have something in my hand, something to grip in case we encounter trouble. I'm swinging the tire iron, lazily, at imaginary opponents as me and Jenna continue heading north.

"If we're where I think we are," I say, looking ahead, "we'll be running into 17 soon, which'll take us east."

"What's east?" she asks. She's hugging herself like a cold-natured person often does.

"Nothing, I guess. I wasn't thinking of anything specific. You said you were headed south, right? Toward New Orleans?"

"Yeah."

"Me and Wes were headed south, too, before we were captured. My family was vacationing in Florida when all that disaster stuff went down, and Wes, well, I don't know much about him. Could you believe him hitting Brad like that?"

"Some people just crack under pressure."

"Still, though."

I look behind me, but there's nothing on the road. I have the feeling someone is following us, but I don't want to scare

Jenna, so I don't mention it. She'll catch on to me eventually, or maybe she'll decide I'm paranoid. There are worse things to be. I take a deep breath, smelling rain and plant life.

"Anyway," I continue, "I'd like to find my family as much as you want to find yours, but I don't think heading south is our best option if we don't want to get caught. We don't have a car, and we'd be walking right past militia central, unless we figure out a way around without losing track of the Interstate."

"We can go east, but do you think we'll ever see Wes or Brad again?"

"I'm not sure," I say. "I'm not sure I want to."

"What's east again?"

"Nothing. Nothing until you hit bigger cities. It seems we should go to a bigger place in a time like this. The conditions will be better, I think, and there will be more supplies. We'll run into more people—hopefully good ones. We may be able to find transportation."

"How long do you think it'll take us to get to a city?"

"On foot? A couple weeks, if we're lucky. We'll have to get food and water along the way, of course. You haven't had much input about all this. Are you sure you're okay with it? Do you have any other ideas?"

"Not really."

"You're not really okay with it, or you don't really have any other ideas?"

"The second one. I just think we should stick together in case something happens. I feel much more comfortable with you around than if I was just by myself."

"Yeah, me too, even though you're a girl." I smile.

"Funny." She smiles back.

By the time we reach the spot where 56 meets 17, we've spent most of the day walking. I'm hungry and thirsty—I'm sure she is also—and I know we'll have to start looking for somewhere to sleep for the night. I've driven through this area before, on one of many family vacations that took us all over this part of the country, so I know not much of 17 will go by without us running into a gas station or even a cluster of them. My fear is that they'll have been looted and demolished after the storms rendered technology useless. All those hunks of metal and miles of wires don't amount to anything anymore. Wes saw the last broadcasts, or so he said. I wish I had.

"Did you hear anything about the natural disasters?" I say. I pick up a small rock and toss it into the woods.

"No. The electricity was out when I left, but I knew something was going on when my car radio didn't pick up any signals."

I-17 is more heavily traveled than where we're originally coming from, so I'm anticipating encountering people, or at least what they left behind, and sure enough, once the junction comes into view, we see several stranded cars that appear as if their owners deserted them. When we get closer, it's a different story.

There's a semi truck, a couple minivans, and a few cars— each heavily damaged. The windows are busted out of most of the vehicles, while the more expensive-looking cars have been stripped. There are a couple bodies lying in the street, right outside what used to be their cars. But me and Jenna wordlessly agree to stay clear of everything, get on 17, and keep walking to wherever we're headed.

"We maybe can use some stuff from those," I say, trying to be practical.

"It's not worth it," Jenna says.

"You're right. We need to find shelter for the night. Food."

"That'd be great. I—we—haven't eaten anything since this morning. Or was it last night?"

"I don't remember. Same difference, I guess. I'm starving."

The sights don't change much when we're off 56. Oftentimes we'll see abandoned cars on the shoulder of the Interstate or in the middle of it. There isn't a soul to be found, which I attribute to fear. I recall the Rapture bumper sticker I've seen so many times: "In case of Rapture, this car will be unmanned." I change the sticker in my mind: In case of Rapture, this car will be unwomanned. In case of Rapture, this car will be unpersonned. Gotta be politically correct these days.

Most sensible people are probably holed up somewhere, hoping order will be restored and everything will shortly return to normal. Those who have Y2K bunkers, or bomb shelters, are finally getting use out of the things, but the ones who are out, I figure, are on the prowl. The only people I think we'll run into are criminals, and maybe other people like ourselves, who don't have anyplace else to go.

"Only two more miles," Jenna says, pointing to the green sign that denotes a future exit. The blue one next to it has icons—one for gas, food, and telephone.

"Maybe we'll get lucky. Who knows?"

Dusk is quickly approaching, and I fear we'll have to sleep outside again with no food. Despite our lack of energy, I suggest we pick up the pace so we can reach the exit with enough daylight to forage. It's foreboding, though. I have a premonition, a bad feeling.

My feet are killing me. They're sore and it hurts to walk. I don't think I could handle running if I tried. The Pit kept us wet, as did the rain, so the first thing I'm gonna do when we get somewhere safe is take off my shoes and socks, let my body dry. I'm going to ditch my clothes as soon as I can. My pants are ruined since I won't be able to wash them. I'll have to find others. It's cool outside, but not enough that it bothers me just yet.

I'm relieved when I see the group of buildings off the exit. There are three gas stations—one appears long abandoned, judging by its dingy façade, broken windows, and littered, weed-strewn parking lot—and what looks like a fast food restaurant, long gone. As we get closer, I can see what we're up against. The second gas station has been ransacked and gutted. Broken glass lies everywhere, shards resting among toppled shelves and crushed goods. Some of the nonperishable items are salvageable—dented cans of vegetables, open packages of Ramen—but the sight of the third gas station gets my hopes up, even though it's boarded up like the owners had been expecting a hurricane. People in Indiana always overreact to the news, but maybe a measure like this isn't an overreaction.

In the open doorway of the ravaged one, I say, "Screw this place. At least we'll have somewhere to sleep that's covered if we need to stay here."

"I suppose," Jenna says. "Broken glass is *so* comfortable."

"True." Normally I'd retort, but I'm preoccupied. "We should try that other one then."

"How?"

"I don't know yet."

Upon closer inspection, the place seems even more impenetrable than I initially thought. Someone hammered so many nails into each sheet of plywood that I lose track trying to count them. As a matter of fact, I don't try since the sun is setting. It's on the horizon now and will dip below it soon. The windows are obviously a no-go, as are the doors. They're locked. Anything that can be smashed is boarded.

"There's gotta be a way to get in there," says Jenna.

"Maybe not," I say and then shrug. I'm not going to give up that easily, though. I think of trying to pry off the plywood boards with the tire iron, but know it'd be futile, and would only tucker me out. More importantly, we can use the station as our fortress if we gain entrance without ruining its defenses.

We walk around the building, slowly, and I'm searching for a clue like I've lost something. Once we get around back, I notice wood sticking out from behind the air conditioner unit. I point and Jenna looks.

"A ladder," I say, pulling it from its hiding spot. It's caked with dirt, and its metal parts are covered with rust. "The roof. Maybe it's worth a shot." I open the ladder and set it parallel to the building—right against the wall. It's about as tall as I am, which is to say not very, so I'm gonna have to jump and then hoist myself onto the roof. Jenna stands where she is, watching while I climb the shaky ladder. I almost ask her to brace it, but decide not to. She'll realize her mistake if I fall, especially off the very top step, the one you're never supposed to stand on. When I'm near the top, I toss the tire iron onto the roof.

The jump's easy. The hard part is pulling myself up when I've gone so long without food and water. I'm sluggish, lethargic, and starving, but wide awake with adrenaline as fuel. I inspect the roof once I'm on it, knowing that if the door or hatch or whatever it's called is locked from the inside, then we won't be able to get in no matter what we do, which will make my prior efforts useless. There's a padlock on the handle. I peer over the building's side.

"You might as well come up here," I say. I walk to the edge to help her. "We'll be safer sleeping up here, out of sight, than on the ground in one of those other stations."

"Fine." Jenna climbs the rickety ladder—probably wary it'll collapse—and I latch onto her arms when she jumps toward the roof.

"We'll be safer up here," I repeat, sitting on the roof with my arms propping me up from behind. She has her knees pulled in close to her body and her arms around herself. We both have to catch our breaths.

"Should we pull the ladder up?"

"Nah, too much trouble. We might need it when we leave. If we can get in that hatch, then we can lock it from the inside so no one'll be able to get in, even if they make it onto the roof. There's a padlock on it. Don't know if I can break it."

"That sucks."

I retrieve the tire iron and grab the lock, positioning it so I can strike it again and again until it breaks off like in the movies. I hit it with all the force I can muster, and eventually, either because I hit the right spot or because it's just plain old, it breaks. The hatch opens, too, which also surprises me.

"Must've forgotten to lock it," she says.

"Yeah, since they went to all this trouble, you'd think they would've locked it. Oh well. Good for us."

The hatch is open and I peer into the darkness below, attempting to determine what's down there to no avail. It's almost dark outside. The sun's barely above the horizon, and I know we have only a few more minutes of daylight.

"There should be a ladder attached that leads down into the store," I say. "I've been on a roof like this before watching fireworks one time. I'll go first."

I position myself and trust my foot will eventually hit a rung. It does. From there I slowly climb into the pitch black station. At the bottom, I tell her it's her turn. When she's on the ladder, I call to her and tell her to close the hatch above. She pulls it shut, like closing a vault door, in spite of its hefty weight.

"Lock it," I say.

"How do I do that?"

"Feel around for a lever, and then pull it whichever direction it'll go. That should lock it. Push up on the hatch afterward to make sure it won't budge. I know it's hard doing it in the dark, but…"

What's with my double entendres lately? "Maybe we'll get lucky"? "I know it's hard doing it in the dark"? I'm glad Jenna hasn't capitalized on them. Soon after, I hear a loud metallic click, which reverberates throughout the building.

"I'm pretty sure it's locked," she says.

"Now try opening it."

"It won't open. The handle won't even turn."

"Okay, cool."

I put my hand on the small of her back, when she's down far enough to reach me, to let her know I have her if she falls. We can't see each other even when she gets down. It's dark as a cave. Since the windows are boarded and the electricity's off with little chance of returning, there's no light whatsoever. I mention that, if everything's still intact, there'll be lighters on the counter, near the register. We can use those for light until we find something better, something more permanent.

I might as well be blind, because I have to resort to feeling around in the dark. Stepping cautiously, I outstretch my hands and finger boxes of candy to my immediate right. I know I've found the impulse buy section next to the counter. I remember pretending I was blind when I was young, except this time, when I open my eyes, there's only darkness. "Blind people must have it rough," I say to Jenna.

"Yeah," she says from behind me.

I inch along, careful to not bump anything that seems like it'll tip over. Later, I find a bin of lighters on the countertop. It takes a few flicks—I'm a nonsmoker—but the flame eventually jumps out of the lighter like a jack-in-the-box.

I study the fire for a couple seconds until I fully come to my senses. I turn around, and though the store's dark, there's enough light to tell that it's been untouched since the owner locked it days ago. To my relief, it's filled to the brim with food and drinks. In one of the aisles I quickly peruse, there are mosquito-repellant candles, so I open one and light it. I set it down on the counter along with the lighter. It reminds me of being around a campfire.

"Let's eat!" I say to Jenna, before smiling from ear to ear, rubbing my hands together as if I'm going to do something illicit. Jenna smiles. I grab a bottle of water from the fridge, which obviously isn't running, and chug it. Maybe it's bad of me, but I don't offer anything to Jenna. Every man for himself, I figure, or every woman for herself. Every person for his or her self.

After the water, I heave a carton of orange juice out and open it. Normally I'll choose milk, but milk goes bad fast, so the juice is the best, healthiest choice.

"Hey," I say. I'm eyeing the carton. "Does orange juice go bad if it gets warm again?"

"I dunno," Jenna says. She's digging through boxes of granola bars while munching on something.

I drink the orange juice, stuff my face with a handful of blueberry Nutri-Grain bars, and then, for dessert, I scarf down several Twinkies, a weakness of mine.

"Now these things...these things last forever," I say through a mouthful of food. Jenna's gulping from a bottle of water. "I ate too fast." I sit down on the tile floor with my back against the counter, but ever so carefully, like a pregnant woman would. Jenna sits down next to me, but about an arm's length away.

"What're we gonna do?" she asks.

"Now?"

"Tomorrow."

"I don't think there's much of a point in staying here. Once we run out of food, which would take forever I'm sure, this place would be useless. Since the windows are all boarded up, we're basically barricaded in here—kind of like jail. We could always hang out on the roof in the daytime, but we'd risk alerting people to our presence if we did that. Right now, you can't tell anyone's in here from the outside. Maybe we should keep going east toward a bigger city. I wanted to go south at first to try and find my family, but it'll take too long without actual supplies and whatnot. We need to find other people so we can protect ourselves."

"Yeah."

"I don't mean to pry," I say, "but what's up? You don't ever talk more than you have to. You want to talk about it?"

She brings her hands to her face and starts crying quietly. It's the inevitable breakdown.

"I'm sorry," she says. Tears leak through the cracks between her fingers and occasionally sprint down her arms.

"No, it's okay. I just...I mean...it's okay. I'm not a very consoling person. Sorry for that." I stare ahead at the displays—food, beer, toiletries, winter accessories, etc.

"I just miss my family. That's all." She's calming down, wiping tears from her face. We're both really dirty from The Pit.

"I do, too. Miss mine, I mean. It's bad, but I can't remember the last thing I said to any of them. I do remember that I told my brother to try to have fun on the vacation."

"What's your brother like?"

"He's young, thirteen. He's at the stage where our parents are the last people he wants to be seen with. He was mad that our dad was making him go with them to Florida but not making me. He doesn't get that I'm a lot older than him."

"He's looking for an excuse to have you around."

"Possibly. I hate to think I'll never see them again. What about your family?"

"I don't want to talk about them," she says. "But thanks for asking."

"Fair enough. If you ever do want to talk about them, I'll be here," I say.

A pessimist through and through, I figure I'll never see my family again, but if I do, I'll be thankful. A part of me is optimistic that life will return to the way it was, that I'll be reunited with my family. We'll build a new house. We'll resume our old lives. A new life doesn't sound that bad, but not this new life.

"I hope you see them again," she says.

"I hope you see yours."

"Thanks."

We both want to get cleaned up, so we carry the candle from room to room looking for the best way and most secluded place to clean ourselves in privacy. There's a washbasin in the storeroom, with a hose hooked up to a nozzle and everything, but when I turn the knob, nothing comes out.

Everything has to be as difficult as possible.

"Welp, looks like we're gonna have to use some of those gallons of water in the fridge to shower." We eye each other in the candlelight. "So, I'll go get some and bring 'em here for you to use. You can go first."

"Okay, thank you. What about shampoo?"

"You can pick that out from one of the shelves. Shampoo, conditioner—I have no idea what you like or what some of that stuff even does."

"Such a guy, huh?"

"Yep."

She smiles faintly. I follow suit. After carrying the jugs into the storeroom and setting Jenna up with her own candle, I get to work on the bedding. At first I consider making only one bed, forcing her to sleep close to me unless she makes another bed herself. I decide that's too sleazy, so I construct two.

Because winter's on its way, there's a display of throw blankets, which I eagerly tear into. I fold each blanket in half, stacking several on top of each other to provide extra padding. I quadruple fold a couple blankets to serve as our respective pillows. It's the exact same arrangement me and Wes had that first night in that other gas station—one person on one side of the double doors and the other person on the other side, our heads closer to the checkout counter than the doors. The windows are boarded, though, so I don't think air seeping in will be a problem.

However many minutes later—I've stopped trying to keep track of time—Jenna emerges from the storeroom.

"Wow," I say, genuinely shocked. "You look great!"

"It fits," Jenna says, smiling. Evidently there are extra uniforms in the storeroom I didn't notice—shirts, pants, everything. It has the Speedway logo on the shirt.

"You even have a nametag!"

JENNIFER, it reads.

"There's a whole box of them back there. Old employees. It's not Jenna, but it's close. Sort of."

"I wonder how many girls there are named Jennifer."

"A lot. It's a popular name."

"Yeah. Let's see—Jennifer Aniston, Jennifer Garner, Jennifer Lopez."

"I don't know any famous Jennas," Jenna says.

"I know one," I say.

"Who?"

"Jenna Jameson."

"Oh."

"How much you wanna bet there isn't an Erik in there?"

"There's probably an Eric in there," she says.

"With a K?"

"Oh, probably not then."

"My turn, I guess. What'd you do with your old clothes?"

"Threw 'em away in the trashcan back there, except for my shoes. Just have to wear those, unless we find other ones somewhere."

"Yep. Couple towels back there?"

"Just a few. I was surprised they had any."

"Be back in a few then," I say, walking to the storeroom. I shut the door behind me.

First I rinse the basin to free it of Jenna's dirt and dead skin. That sends me back to a memory from when I went away to college for a little while. The community showers were off-putting for a number of reasons—the threat of athlete's foot being the worst. I never showered without wearing sandals. After zoning out, I peel off my filthy clothes and lay them in a wastebasket nearby. There isn't any way to salvage them. I don't need to, nor do I want to. I think about it for a second. That pile of clothes is the last thing I have from home. I recall my home, empty, but fling that memory out of my head. Maybe I should keep them.

Then, naked, I step into the basin and pour the room temperature water all over me. It isn't nearly as refreshing as the constant stream of a hot shower, but it's nice nevertheless. I wash my hair first, and afterward, my body. Rinsing is a pain because I have to pour water over certain parts, plus, the jugs are heavy until only a little water remains in them. I grab a towel from the metal shelves and dry off, tossing it to the floor right after because I don't think I'll be using it again, as if I'm in a hotel and housekeeping will pick it up during their next go-around.

I rummage through a pile of uniforms for my sizes. Eventually I uncover a shirt and a pair of pants that fit, so I don them in addition to a pair of balled-up socks that were sleeping near the larger items of clothing. I discover an ERIC nametag and pin it to my shirt despite the difference in spelling.

"Awesome," I say to Jenna when I appear, holding my arms at my sides with my palms face up, as if to ask, How do I look? Good? I know.

"Not bad," she says. Jenna's sitting on her makeshift bed, which she chose herself. I lie on mine.

"Yeah, not bad," I say. "You tired?"

"Yeah."

"Should we leave a candle lit?"

"We can. The bathroom would be the best place for it probably. It won't distract us in there. It would help us find it if one of us has to use it during the night. Speaking of, the toilet doesn't flush, so we might want to go number two elsewhere."

"Right. Goodnight, Erik, and thanks."

"For what?"

"For helping. For helping me."

"You're welcome," I say. "And thank you."

"For what?"

"For just being here, I guess. Following me instead of the other guys. Safety in numbers. Two heads are better than one."

"That's okay. Light that candle, though, if you wouldn't mind."

By the time I steal a candle off the shelf, light it, and place it on the sink in the bathroom, Jenna's asleep. I return to the bathroom and stare at myself in the mirror. The only illumination comes from the candle's small flame, which the mirror reflects. The more mirrors, the more light. In the near dark, I look sinister. I strike a pose, bare my teeth like I'm Wolverine or Batman. That leads me to question Wes and his whereabouts, and, to a lesser extent, Brad's. I misread Wes, or at least figure I had. It bothers me since I pride myself on being a good judge of character. I left Brad. What does that say about my character? What does that say about Jenna's? It was the situation. He was knocked out cold. He was too heavy to carry. We couldn't risk getting caught again. If we had more time, it would've been different. I think.

I decide not to dwell on these thoughts. Rather, I walk out to the shelves and search for toothpaste and a toothbrush. I catch myself comparing prices, thinking I'll buy a mid-price toothbrush until I remember I can take whatever I want. Should I leave a note listing what we've eaten? I don't have any cash, nor the means to procure any, but if I leave my clothes here, they could be washed. That'd be a fair exchange, wouldn't it? I pluck a toothbrush off the rack and a box of toothpaste from the lower shelf, a bottle of water from the broken fridge. In the bathroom, I brush my teeth, spit into the sink, and discard the packaging in the wastebasket on the floor.

Normally I'd read a book for an hour before trying to sleep, but that's too impractical in these conditions and I don't have a book, so instead, I tiptoe in and lie down.

"Aw, man," I utter through chattering teeth while shivering and hugging myself to keep warm. "Why's it so cold in here?" I ask myself. It's pitch black, like coffee, wherever I am. I hear a snap then immediately afterward, a billion fluorescent lights ignite overhead. Frost clings to every bulb. Some have icicles. The hallway I'm in has an ice floor—transparent like glass—and below there's nothing but darkness. There's nothing to either side of me either.

"I don't normally show people this," says a voice I recognize. I whip around to behold Jesus, once again. "I'll make an exception for you."

"Too...cold," I tell Him. Every breath drifts into the air visibly, like fog, and soon dissipates. He snaps His fingers, which restores my warmth, making me impervious to the temperature. I'm neither warm nor cold.

"You won't feel the cold unless I let you."

"Cool. That's fine with me," I say. I don't intend the pun. "Hard to walk on this ice, though." He snaps again, furnishing me with sleek ice-skates.

"Follow Me."

He walks down the hallway, which I can tell leads into a larger room, though I'm still too far away to tell what or who's in it. I skate slowly and carefully because I'm scared I'll slip and fall off the side, never to be heard from again, like those explorers who meet death at the bottom of chasms.

"Uh, where are we?" I ask, extending my arms for balance in tightrope walker fashion.

"Don't worry. You won't fall off."

"Good."

We reach the mouth of the room, but I'm not prepared for what I bear witness to. Lined in parallel rows are millions of people lying on individual blocks of ice while giant air conditioners blast cold air down from the ceiling. Some people are naked and some have blankets covering their bodies, but all are shivering as if enduring an eternal seizure.

"Welcome to Hell," Jesus says. We both look on. "The greatest show on Earth. Well, not Earth, but you get the point."

"What's the difference between the people with blankets and the ones without 'em?" I ask.

"Oh, those blankets were soaked in cold water prior, so they make it even colder for them. The people with blankets were extra bad, extra evil."

"So this is Hell?"

"Sort of."

"What do You mean?"

"This is about half of it. You see, people dread either extreme cold or extreme heat and that determines which division of Hell someone will end up in. In fact, it's impossible for a person to fear both equally. So, if you fear fire, brimstone, and being burned alive more, you'll be sent to the fiery pit. If you fear hypothermia, frostbite, and all that jazz, you'll end up in this winter wonderland here."

"Which one would I go to?"

"I think you know the answer to that."

"Yeah, I do. Can I see the other one?"

"Not yet," Jesus says in a foreboding tone. "Maybe some other time." He snaps His fingers, and instantly it's dark and I'm freezing. I wake, but the chills continue to shake my body.

It's just a dream. They're all just dreams, I think in an effort to calm myself. My hope is that I didn't catch a fever during the night. Just in case, I'll grab some Advil tomorrow, before I leave.

# CHAPTER SIX:
# WES KILLS JENNA

L ight creeps in through the cracks, but not enough to fully wake me. I wake on my own, naturally, hoping we haven't slept till the afternoon. I don't want to wait around. It seems like I'm in limbo already, and that me and Jenna aren't making much progress, even if our destination isn't set.

I get out of bed, pick up another candle off the shelf, and go to the bathroom. I flick the light switch out of habit, but when nothing happens, I remember there's no power. I fish the lighter out of my pocket and light the new candle. The other one burnt out overnight.

When I finish, I zip up, and again, out of habit, I pull down the flush handle but nothing happens. I decide to test the sink just to see what will happen, if anything. I go to the sink and turn the H knob to no result.

"Shit," I say quietly. I return to the shelves and browse them for some of that Purell hand sanitizer stuff. *Kills 99.9% of germs!* the packaging boasts. Yeah, right. Oh well. Better than nothing. Plus, who knows? It could be true.

"Good morning," Jenna says. She's still lying in her makeshift bed.

"Morning," I say, "Or maybe afternoon."

"I don't know either."

"Not much point in trying to figure out what time it is. I'm sure there are some watches in here with the date and time, if you really wanna know."

"No, I'm fine."

"Doesn't really matter anymore, I guess."

Jenna gets up and walks to the bathroom. The candle I lit moments ago is still burning. I walk to the cooler to grab a Diet Coke out of the fridge. So many types of one drink. I'll try this Diet Coke Plus. It has vitamins and minerals. That's better than nothing. It's warm, but still tastes great. After a couple big gulps, I put it down and grab a carton of orange juice as well as a handful of various kinds of protein bars made by PowerBar. I sit down to eat.

Jenna emerges from the bathroom. I hold the hand sanitizer in the air and she takes it, squirting some in her hands and rubbing it in.

"Thanks," she says. "Breakfast?" She nods toward my stash.

"Yep. About as good as it gets. Around here, anyway."

She disappears down an aisle while I remain seated against one of the store's double doors. She reappears with some granola bars and an orange juice, then sits down next to me in front of the other door.

"So, we should pack some stuff and head out," I say.

"Pack what?" she asks with a mouthful of food lodged in one cheek, a half chipmunk.

"Food, drinks, stuff."

"What're we gonna put it in?"

"Oh, we'll just get a couple garbage bags or something. Double bag it, of course."

Having finished my meal, I get up and walk to the bathroom to brush my teeth. The toothbrush and toothpaste I'd swiped from the store are on the commode, in addition to a bottle of water I'd set there the previous night. I use it to rinse. Afterward, I walk down the short hallway to the storeroom, where me and Jenna bathed, and scan the racks for a box of garbage bags, which I find.

When I come back into the main room, Jenna's gathered an assortment of stuff like snacks, drinks, and toiletries, so I scoop it up and toss it in the bag, handful by handful. Then I open the other garbage bag, and put it over the other one.

"Nothing's getting in here," I say. I pat the bag.

"I think I'm gonna take a shower," Jenna says.

"Have fun. After you're finished, I think we'll be ready to go."

"Okay. Say, what do you wanna do with this place?"

"Meaning?"

"I mean, lock it up, leave it open?" she asks.

"I guess leave it open. Well not opened, but unlocked. Someone else may need to get in here. The only way we'd be able to stop anyone from getting in here would be to get rid of that ladder out back since we can't lock the roof hatch from the outside."

"Or put the ladder on the roof."

"Yeah, it's probly not worth the trouble."

Minutes later, Jenna's in the storeroom bathing while I sit against the counter playing with a lighter. I flick it again and again, imagining what it would be like to set a fire on purpose, to set a building on fire like an arsonist. I remember that I have. I recollect setting the fire in my house. I wonder how long it took to burn the whole thing down. What did it look like after? Would anything survive the fire? If so, would it be worth returning to the site?

A clanging sound—metal on metal—rouses me from my daydream. At once I know someone's on the roof, trying to get in.

"Jenna, get dressed!" I yell as I pass the storeroom on my way to the ladder, which leads to the rooftop. I know the hatch is locked, momentarily comforting me. We made sure of that last night. Minutes elapse. I freeze like a wax figure, listening for who's out there. Jenna comes out of the storeroom fully clothed, but is drying her hair with a towel.

"What's wrong, Erik?"

"Someone's on the roof."

"What? Who?!"

"I dunno. I heard clanging, like they were trying to pry their way in."

"It's locked, right? From in here?"

"Yeah. There's no way they're getting in here from up there. It'd be impossible."

"Good. I'm gonna finish drying my hair."

"Okay," I say, "I'll just stand here and keep worrying."

I walk back into the main room, wishing I had X-ray vision like Superman so I can see who's lurking out there. But if I had X-ray vision, would I only be able to see their skeleton? Then my attention turns to the boarded-up windows. The light's temporarily blocked when the guy—I assume it's a guy—walks around the front of the building. That's how I figured out how to tell someone's standing in front of a door if it's dark. If it's darker on your side than theirs, their feet will block the light. It happens all the time in the movies. Jenna walks back in.

"What do we do?" she asks.

"I don't know." I'm thinking. "My gut tells me we should stay put for the time being and see if whoever it is just goes away. At least that's what I hope he does."

"Fine then. We'll wait."

We sit and lean against the counter, but don't say much. Time goes by. I'm not sure how much. I don't try to keep track, but start to think maybe I should. Even people marooned on deserted islands keep track of time, usually.

"You smell smoke?" I ask Jenna later.

"I think so. Where's it coming from?"

"I can't tell." Then, at the window to the very left, flames leap up the board that covers the glass. "Shit! The building's on fire!" We both jump to our feet, and Jenna grabs the bag full of our supplies. It's too heavy for her to carry by herself, so I help carry it to the back of the building. "We'll go out through the roof!"

"What about the guy?!"

"We gotta go!"

I drop my part of the bag, climb the ladder, unlock the latch, and push up on the hatch. It barely moves. I push again, with all the might my right arm can muster since my left has to hold onto the ladder. There's too much resistance from the outside. It's not going to open. I climb down frantically.

"What's wrong?" Jenna asks at the bottom.

"It's not gonna open."

"How come?"

"I don't know."

And then it hits me: I left the tire iron on the roof. Whoever it is isn't trying to get in. They're trying to trap us, and burn the place down. The tire iron must be lodged in the hatch's handle to keep us in. "Shit," I say, disgusted with myself and the situation.

"How're we gonna get outta here, Erik?! We gotta get out now!"

I spy a fire extinguisher hanging on the wall, so I grab it and rush to the entrance. I try spraying the fire, but nothing comes out, which means I have to resort to other tactics. My first hit shatters the door's upper pane of glass, and my second, the lower. The fire's spreading. I bang at the long sheet of plywood like a battering ram. With each blow, I feel the sheet give a little more. Finally the sheet falls to the ground outside, and daylight, like an explosion, bursts through the newly made gap. I lean down to exit through the bottom, helping Jenna, who's dragging our bag of supplies, out immediately afterward. We start hacking as if we'd just tried smoking for the first time, but I doubt we inhaled enough smoke to hurt us.

We keep coughing, trying to rid our lungs of the noxious, toxic fumes. I stand with my hands on my knees, bent over. Jenna's next to me, and I can see her shoes in my peripheral vision. She lets go of the bag.

The shot's deafening, and I feel the urge to cover my ears, despite the fact that the damage has already been inflicted. Jenna drops beside me. I look at her body for only a second before turning away. Still, her eyes—radiating fear—will stick with me. It doesn't seem real.

I raise my head to see Wes several yards in front of me. His arm is still extended with the gun pointed where he aimed. We remain silent. I stand upright then, and Wes lowers the gun. We're both calm, as if asking ourselves, So what happens next? Wes, I notice, looks filthier—crazed, even—than when I last saw him. Suddenly, I put it together. I glance over at the gas station, which is burning uncontrollably by this point, and back at Wes. I envision the scenario as part of a movie, and wonder where the film crew hid the cameras, and how they hid them so well.

"You tried to kill us?" I ask. "Why?"

"There wasn't supposed to be anybody else, Erik. Just you," Wes answers.

"Did you go back and kill Brad after we left him?"

"Maybe."

"What're you afraid of? Why won't you just admit it? It's not like you're gonna get arrested or anything. I mean, look around. Look at where we are!" I motion toward the rapidly burning gas station, which I expect to explode due to the chemical agents inside. I stand my ground, though. "Look at where we are, man! This is the fucking apocalypse!"

"No, Erik. No it's not. You fantasize about doing things to people, Erik? Stealing from them? Raping them? Killing them?"

"Where'd you get the gun?" I ask, attempting to stall and change the subject at the same time.

"Doesn't matter now, does it?"

"So, I guess it's my turn, huh? Brad's outta the way. Jenna's gone. That leaves me. They were good people, by the way, or Jenna was at least."

"They were in the wrong place at the wrong time, but I enjoyed the practice. I'm a hunter, Erik. A mercenary. My boss would've been able to use you. Before these disasters happened, you would've lived on, sort of. Your organs in other people's bodies. Now you're just gonna die."

"What are you talking about?" I ask.

"Black market. Your organs. Figured I'd run into a hitchhiker after the disasters. I'd kill you and take you back to my boss for an easy payday. But, things got fucked up. They do that sometimes. Now, with no transportation and no place to store your body, this is just a game. Now the fun begins. Now you know I'm chasing you."

"Why are you telling me this?"

"Shit ain't worth doing if you don't get the credit for it. Now you know who you're up against."

"Let's just get this over with."

"Okay. You're free then. You're free to go."

"What?"

"Get outta here." He nods his head to the right, signaling the direction he wants me to take. "Into the woods over there."

Past the field behind the trio of gas stations, the woods resume. For some reason he wants me to continue heading east—the direction I've been heading ever since escaping The Pit. The clearing won't take too long to traverse, and I'll be staying parallel to the Interstate for a while, so I figure what the hell. Resting beside Jenna's feet is the garbage bag we filled with food, water, and other stuff. I bend over, grab it, and sling it over my shoulder.

"Leave it," Wes tells me.

"Fuck you," I say. I can hear Wes coughing as I begin walking toward the woods. A few seconds after his coughing dissipates, I look back, but he's already gone. Why'd he let me live?

When I reach the woods' edge, I turn and look again. The burning gas station is beyond help—not that any help is on the way. My family and friends are probably dead. Jenna's dead. Nonetheless, I feel compelled to try and survive. I step into the woods thinking I might not make it back out.

Ever since the weather took a turn for the worst, the sky's been overcast whenever it isn't raining. The clouds are always gray and ominous, as if saturated with rain and ready to burst at any moment. Resembling a gas station employee who's abandoned his post, since I'm still wearing the garb I slept in, I trudge through the wild until I get thirsty, whereupon I sit against a tree, reach into the bag, and pull out a bottle of water. Usually I guzzle. Thinking it could be worse, things do get worse when, with no warning whatsoever, the clouds empty their contents. The rain flies down in sheets, soaking me thoroughly within a matter of minutes. It reminds me of summer days when it'll be sunny, then it'll rain, then it'll be sunny again, then it'll rain some more, and so on. Still, there's no thunder or lightning, which I find strange. Sitting there as wet as can be, I suddenly get pissed off.

"Fuck you!" I shout at the sky, but to nothing in particular. "And fuck you, too!" I yell at the garbage bag, heaving it as far as I can from my sitting position. Then, only a minutes after it started, the rain stops. If we slept until the afternoon, I've only got a few more hours until dark. I rise, shoulder the garbage bag, and resume hiking to wherever I'm going.

It's odd how revelations come to me out of nowhere, seemingly triggered by nothing. Wes is hunting me. I recall *The Most Dangerous Game*, a story turned movie about a hunter who'd hunted everything except what would prove the most challenging—a fellow human. I can't remember how it ended, though, which I consider unnerving. There's no logical reason why he killed everyone around me, unless he wanted me to be alone with only my wits to survive.

He probably figured I'd be the most difficult to kill. Out of Brad, Jenna, and me, I guess I am. That isn't saying much. According to Wes, he hadn't ever intended to kill anyone except me. After all, Jenna and Brad were thrown into The Pit before we escaped, so he had to take them out in order to take me out.

I unclip my ERIC nametag and toss it into the air. Maybe someone will find it someday, and wonder who ERIC was, what he was doing out here, and why he ditched his nametag. Maybe they'll create him for themselves, imagining what he was like and what he liked to do. I smile at the thought, reminding myself I'd done the same thing a thousand times when I was people-watching at the mall.

Occasionally I get hungry. When I do, I reach in the bag and produce a PowerBar, Nutri-Grain, or whatever else is in there. Instead of littering, I deposit all my trash back in the bag. Maybe the world is ending, but that's still no excuse to litter. Even so, I could never bring myself to litter except when it came to banana peels and apple cores. There's simply no justification for it. If I finish with the garbage bag, which is unlikely because it has so many potential uses, I plan to bury it somewhere out of the way. It's biodegradable.

I consider keeping an eye on the Interstate while I walk so I never get too far from the beaten path, but shrug off the notion when I remind myself that it doesn't really matter where I'm headed. I assume the chances of getting lost are slim to none. The woods can't be that dense. It's not like it's a forest.

Gravity hits me: I don't know where to go and I'm going to die. I think of my family and friends, whose fates I don't know and won't find out. I don't cry. I force myself not to. Crying won't accomplish anything. What will accomplish something is a plan, a plan to live, so that's what I craft. I will kill Wes. I will live on. I will find my family or I will die trying. I will keep moving.

Hours later the sun's going down—not that I can see it through the clouds—and I feel a sting of panic at the prospect of sleeping outside in the rain, with no solution in sight. Even though it factored into Wes's plan, if he's indeed hunting me, every waking moment should be spent moving. Other than sleep, I have to keep my ultimate goals in mind. Sitting around won't do me good in any respect. As long as I've got supplies, I'll be all right. I've got to find a weapon.

So, with twilight setting in on the landscape, I find a nice, thick tree to lean against. I remove a throw blanket from the garbage bag and place it on the ground, as well as a rolled-up one to serve as my pillow. I also take out a flashlight, and the only reading material I have—a state map Jenna packed. I know that once it's unfolded, I'll never be able to get it back together, but I study it anyway. I wish for a "You are here" dot.

Amazingly, I remember the Interstate and exit number, so I have a rough idea of where I am, even though I'm not that familiar with the area despite its proximity to my home.

"Whoa," I say when I see just how thick the woods seem on the map. "There's probly nothing for miles."

Still, I have no way of knowing precisely where I am, so I bunch the map up as best I can, then slide it back into the bag. The flashlight I turn off, but keep in my hand. There's nothing to do except hope it won't rain again. Thankfully, it doesn't. After a while, I close my eyes, and suffering the hard, uncomfortable ground, I manage to drift off for a few hours.

I'm in a massive parking lot filled with a sea of miniature cars. I see neon-infused structures in the distance, like those found in most theme parks. I hear faint circus music.

"What the?"

"Meowland."

"What? Who said that?"

It's dark in the lot, but I scrutinize my surroundings for the voice.

"Over here. To your left." It's the mother kitten on the roof of a mini-car. Her tail's wagging.

"Hey," I say, and smile. "You blend in so well, being all black."

"Welcome to Meowland."

"What's Meowland?"

She jumps off the car and begins trotting toward the entrance, which seems miles away.

"Meowland is the greatest place on Earth for cats and kittens."

"Say, how've you been?" I ask. I'm attempting to pry and maybe get some information about what's going on, or what else is going to happen.

"Better than you."

"You're right, I'm sure. I've been having a hard time lately. Hey, slow down a bit."

"Oh, sure. Sorry. When you have four legs, it's easy to get carried away."

"Yeah, plus your ankles don't have to dodge all these rearview mirrors like I do, having to walk in between all these parked mini-cars."

Eventually we reach the entrance and other than the cat theme, it's like any amusement park. There are miniature turnstiles that the cats and kittens are forced through, in addition to signage that points out various rules, amenities, and rides. My favorite sign is the "No Dogs" one, which looks like a "No Smoking" sign. I look up at the banner above us. MEOWLAND, it flashes in bright, neon lettering. Above that is a cat's face also accentuated with neon. All the while, typical carnival music pours out of hidden speakers. I smell turkey being cooked.

"Can I go in?"

"Normally no, but they're gonna make an exception this time, considering the circumstances."

"What circumstances?"

"Your death," the mother says offhandedly, darting to one of the turnstiles. They're built for cats, while even smaller ones are made to suit kittens. I approach the row of turnstiles, feeling like a giant out of *Gulliver's Travels* or *Honey, I Blew up the Kid*. "I already paid for you," she says, "so just step on over."

I step over the turnstiles, careful to not smash any paws or tails beneath my shoes. There are cats of all colors and sizes. Families are obvious due to color scheme, and size to a certain extent, but Meowland is littered with so many felines it's impossible to keep track of any of them for very long.

Once I'm inside the park, I notice more signs denoting LITTERBOXES and FOOD. I assume I'm too big, and too structurally different, to ride any of the rides, and I'm right. The rollercoasters look fun, especially the ones called "The Canine" and "The Skinner," but there's no way for me to ride them. Instead, we walk around, looking at all the games and vendors cats set up to con other cats out of their hard-earned catnip. There are milk shooting games where you try to shoot a scrolling hunter, mice races where you can bet on which mouse will win the race, and mock catfights where two robotic beasts are pitted against one another a la Rock 'Em Sock 'Em Robots.

"Are you hungry?" the mother asks me later.

"Not really. What do you all have to eat?"

"Not much you'll like, I'm afraid. We've got cat food, mice, chicken, turkey, and different kinds of fish. Fried mice kebobs are Meowland's specialty."

"Like I said, I'm not very hungry. Thanks, though."

In walking around, I find myself being stared at a number of times—too many to count. We reach the edge of the park, which is oddly secluded. Full-size beds are set up at various places, similar to our benches, so cats can relax beside milk fountains. I sit on the edge of the bed. The mother kitten sits next to me, and since we parted however many days ago, I feel weird about petting her, so I refrain. I especially feel weird because she can talk. We can hear all the carnival sounds—rides, games, meows—in the background.

"It's getting close," she says.

"What're you talking about?"

"To the end. Yours."

"Will I go out in a blaze of glory?" I ask, joking because I'm not sure how serious the news is, or how to take it. How does one deal with such information anyway? Not knowing the future is the whole appeal of living. If we know what's going to happen, what would be the point in seeing those events through? How could you hope things would get better if you knew they weren't going to?

"No."

"Listen, there are a couple things I don't understand. One, Jesus keeps appearing in my dreams—which, I guess this is only one, but whatever—and He's kind of a jerk."

"You haven't figured it out yet?" she asks.

"Figured what out?"

"He's not really Jesus. He's just your mind's perception of Him. Your projection of Him. You don't really know Him at all."

"That makes sense. What about that horse? That white horse appears, too. Lately I haven't killed him, but in earlier dreams, I did. What is he? What's he there for? What's he want?"

"Why don't you ask him yourself?"

With her tail she points to the gate a few yards in front of us. In the distance is the white horse, staring at me.

"Hey!" I stand up. The horse turns and runs away into the cover of darkness. "Hey! Wait a minute." I sit back down on the bed, propping myself up with my hands behind me. "He won't ever just stay put, you know? He always runs away. Or is too far away in the first place."

"You're not supposed to meet yet."

"How do you know all this stuff?"

"I don't know. I really don't."

There's a lightning strike in the distance, like a silent whip, and then thunder. The mother kitten looks aloft, as do I.

"It's gonna rain," I say.

"This is the last time I'll see you, so think about what the horse is associated with, and there you'll find your answer—what he is, what he wants. Good luck, and goodbye."

She hops off the bed, and breaks into a full speed run. Before long, I lose track of her. Cats retreat to awnings and the insides of buildings while thunder continues to sound off and lightning bolts from sky to ground. The rains come. As I'm sitting here getting drenched, I look back at Meowland. Places that are supposed to be crowded are creepy when they're empty. It's eerie, but the rain rouses me from sleep, a rain which soaks me from head to toe, even though I'm splayed on the ground like I've been murdered, with my limbs pointing every which way, as if marking the directions to several, nearby cities.

D ammit."
        I shift to my side to try and get more comfortable, then I pull the last blanket out of the garbage bag to shield my head from the rain. It's a dumb move. I should've left it in the bag, so it'll be dry in the morning when I need to towel off. It's still dark out. The downpour didn't last long, and thus it's possible for me to get a few more hours of sleep, if I can manage. Somehow, I do. Maybe I'm more exhausted than I thought, because the cold, hard wet ground doesn't lend itself to sleep, nor does the absence of proper, dry bedding. I wake in the morning to overcast skies yet again. Some sleep is always better than none. I get up and stretch like I'm reaching for the clouds in order to palm a couple.

As always, the first thing I do in the morning is pee. There's a roll of toilet paper in the bag, so I take a crap and pile the toilet paper and bury it with dirt, leaves, and twigs. It'll decompose quickly, I assume. Is that the right word? Essentially, the garbage bag functions as a portable convenience store, so naturally there's also a toothbrush and a tube of toothpaste in it. I brush my teeth and rinse with water from a bottle. There isn't much water left, which means I'll have to not only conserve by monitoring my intake, but also set the empties out to catch the rain. I eat some granola bars afterward, bundle up the blankets, and ship off to an undetermined destination.

For a majority of the day, I walk through the woods, occasionally pausing to relieve myself in one or more ways. The hottest part of the day comes and goes during which nothing notable happens. Until, that is, I approach the lake. First there's a clearing, but a sizeable hill blocks the view. Once I scale the hill, I see the lake, panoramic in scope. Unless I want to swim across, I have no choice but to walk its perimeter until I reach the other side.

"How'd I not know about all this?" I ask myself out loud.

I set the bag on the ground, and dig out the crumpled mess of a map. Yep. Sure enough there's a lake however many miles to the southeast of where I started out, after departing from the scene at the gas station. I swear the lake wasn't as big on the map last night. At the moment I seem to be in a spot people don't usually frequent—there's not a trace of empty bottles or cans, paper, etc.—but I notice a dock in the distance, to my left, so I walk toward it. I leave my bag unattended.

I get to the dock, walk to the end of it, and face the lake. It spans quite a distance, other than the few small islands dotting its surface. I briefly wonder if it's manmade, but dismiss the thought considering its unusual shape. Evening will be here before I know it. The sun's in the sky somewhere, but still gray, foreboding clouds obscuring it from view. There are ripples here and there, though the water is remarkably calm. The calm before the storm, as they say. I turn to make my way around the rest of the lake.

# CHAPTER SEVEN:
# WES VERSUS ERIK

At the end of the dock, where it meets grass, is the white horse, motionless. I stand my ground, too, yet blink more than I normally do while I try to ascertain whether the horse is an illusion, mirage, or daydream.

You aren't real, I think. This can't be real.

"So," I say, pausing. "The mother, er, someone told me I could figure out why you're following me if I know what I associate you with. In my first dreams, I killed you, and after the other ones, other people died in real life. So I guess what I associate you with is death."

The horse continues to block the way, but only looks in my direction. It doesn't react. It's like I've said nothing at all. Suddenly, my brain's connecting threads and concepts.

"I hate horses. Always have. You knew that, didn't you? I'm next then. That's what all this means. Someone's gonna die. There's no one left but me. I'm gonna die."

The horse turns and runs over the hill as if spooked. I know there's nothing else I need to find out to be at ease, except for the whereabouts of my family and friends, who I'm positive I'll never see again. And my cats. Then, almost as if on cue, Wes walks down the hill and commandeers the spot the horse previously occupied, holding the pistol at his side.

"I expected more from you, Erik, but you've done enough running. I've given you plenty of opportunities to escape, and you've botched every one of them. This is quickly becoming dull, and it's time to move on to more exciting and challenging things."

"Killing other people?"

"Yes."

"You didn't give me much of a chance here."

"You didn't even try to cover your tracks! I was able to follow your trail. The nametag? The buried toilet paper? Sloppy, Erik, sloppy. You got far, in light of the circumstances. I have to admit The Pit was a low that even I didn't expect to escape from, but you did good there. Made it easy on me."

"Let's just get this over with. If you're going to kill me, then do it."

I'm on the edge of the dock, looking at the water, and my back is turned to Wes, who is probably raising the gun. The clouds still block the sun. I think about trying to escape somehow. I recall the episode of a TV show during which they tested the accuracies of guns when shot into a pool of water. They proved that bullets of all calibers lose their momentum as fast as they gain it, rendering their attacks useless if the target is adequately submerged.

I take a deep breath and I dive as far out into the cold, murky lake as possible, praying the lack of visibility and odd angle will nullify Wes's efforts.

The first shot rings out but I don't feel anything. The water's flooding my ears, muffling all sound, including the second shot. And the third. And the fourth. Then it's quiet. My breath is almost gone and I need to resurface, but I force myself to swim a little farther down in case Wes is awaiting the inevitable. Finally, when I can't hold my breath any longer, I look up and open my eyes. Through the blurriness

I can distinguish the dock above, because the water is darker there, so I plan to surface right under it, giving Wes a harder shot.

At the surface the water runs down my face as I loudly inhale the oxygen that will keep me alive for at least another moment. I wipe my eyes and look to my left and right. Wes is on the shoreline, a mere stone's throw away, and he tests this when he hurls the gun at my head, the only part of me above water, but misses. I watch the firearm sink until it disappears.

Out of ammo. The only possible explanation.

Wes makes for the dock like he's going to try and drag me out of the water, but his cough brings him to his knees, then to all fours. I swim to the shore and pull myself out, knowing we're on a level playing field now that he's been disarmed. We're both tired—him from coughing, me from swimming. I'm not a violent person, but I know what I have to do.

I walk out to the dock and kick Wes in the stomach as hard as I can. Water droplets fall off me like tiny bombs. He groans in pain and lies on his side. I kick again. I kick, move to his face, kick him there. I kick him until my foot hurts. I kick him until my foot and his face are covered in blood. I kick him until he's not trying to resist, until he stops moving. I watch his chest rise and fall, so I know he's still breathing.

I don't want to do it—even after what Wes has done—but I convince myself that I have to. I lean down and push him toward the end of the dock. At the end of it, I make sure he lands face down in the water. He drowns, but unconsciously. There's no struggle.

I sit down and lean against one of the dock's poles. I'm breathing heavily, starting to chill from the cold water. It feels like the end, but I know it's only the beginning. Everything is lost—my family, my friends, my pets, my book.

"The safe. Why the fuck didn't I think of the safe?" I say, astounded that I could forget something like that.

In my parent's bedroom there's a fireproof safe bolted to the floor. It's too heavy for one person to carry, and even if a few people were able to cart it off, they wouldn't be able to open it without a safecracker or industrial-strength tools. I know the combination.

When Dad set me down the night he told me the combo, he said, "You and me. We're the only ones who know the combination. Not even your Mom knows it."

"What's in it?" I asked.

"Supplies for emergencies. A gun. I'll teach you how to use it, but you can't tell your Mom. She thinks there aren't any guns in the house. Never, under any circumstances, do you open that safe unless it's a dire emergency and you can't reach me. Understand?"

I said I did. Other things in the safe: bullets and cash. That is, if everything's still there since I last checked, a few years ago, when my parents and siblings went out for the night and I was curious. This counts as a "dire emergency," I think.

I couldn't have gone that far from home. I'll circle back, find the safe among the rubble, and gather the last of our belongings. I'll head south to find my family. If I don't make it, at least I tried.

I get up and walk onto the shore where I pick up the bag. Daylight is waning, but I rifle through the bag looking for anything I can drop to make my load lighter. I throw out a few protein bar wrappers and anything else I don't think I'll need. The sensible thing would be to look for a place to crash for the night and build a small fire to keep warm, but I'm too anxious for that, so I take out the map. I figure out the general direction of my house and start walking, determined to live, to stay alive. Survive.

# SPECIAL THANKS

Thanks to my family, friends, and fellow writers—you know who you are. Thanks, especially, to Christy Diulus, Karen Goldman, and Aubrey Hirsch for their input, which made this book a whole lot better than it originally was.